BOSTON

HOMICIDE

BY

John C. Dalglish

2015

BOSTON HOMICIDE

MONDAY, NOVEMBER 1

BOSTON MEDICAL CENTER
SOUTH BOSTON
12:30 A.M.

Cary Brennan pulled her jacket tighter as she waited at the bus stop in front of Boston Medical Center. Her midnight shift just having ended, she was repeating the nightly ritual of riding the bus to Andrew Station, followed by a connection that took her to 4th Street in South Boston. She then walked the block and a half to her home.

Shortly, the MBTA bus pulled up and she climbed on. As usual, there were only a few other riders, and her customary seat behind the driver was open. It was only fifteen minutes to Andrew Station, and she passed the time with her Kindle reader and the latest Nora Roberts romance. She reached Andrew Station just in time to make her connection, then watched out the window as South Boston scrolled by.

Southie had recently gone through a building boom. The new waterfront complex and many upscale shops were among the changes occurring since Cary had moved into the area. She inherited her parent's row house, and with the boom in property values, she felt lucky to be able to stay in the area. On her nurse's salary, she could never afford to buy there, but she'd moved in to care for her mother in the last days of her life. The refurbished row house had become hers when her mom passed last year.

Her stop came and she climbed out into the chill of the late November night air. Temperatures now hovered in the low forties when she went home each night, and she already longed for summer to return. It wasn't just the warmth, but each night she would pass people sitting on the front porches, waving or stopping to say hi. Now, houses were closed up against the chill and the coming Boston winter.

It was only a block and a half from her stop to her front door, and she hurried along the side street with her shoulders hunched against the wind. She didn't hear the car come up behind her.

"Hey!"

Cary turned to see an unfamiliar vehicle stop by the curb. The window was open on the passenger side. "Cary... Cary Brennan, right?"

Cary stooped over to look into the car. "Yeah?"

"Remember me?"

The interior light came on, and Cary got her first look at the driver. "Oh yeah, of course."

"Have you got a minute?"

She moved closer. "I guess, why?"

He put the car in park and got out. "I wanted to show you something."

Suddenly, her instincts were screaming at her to run for home, and to her boyfriend who was waiting for her. She never got the chance to obey them.

PRECINCT C-6
9:00 A.M.

Danny Sullivan pulled into the parking lot across Broadway from Southie Precinct C-6 headquarters. A red brick structure, it was non-descript, meshing seamlessly with the factories and shops in the area.

Taking a quick look in his rearview mirror, Danny ran his hand through his sandy brown hair. Combined with his pale green eyes, it was hard to pick up his Irish heritage. He'd been spared the freckles of his brother and sister, and only when he hadn't shaved for a few days did his family bloodline start to show. His beard was flaming red.

Deciding he looked as good as possible, he went inside the precinct. His nine a.m. meeting with the lieutenant was at hand, and he was having a hard time concealing his frayed nerves. After all, if he got the promotion, he'd be the first in his family to make detective.

His wife, Cassie, had climbed out of bed early this morning, fixing him breakfast and doing her best to calm him down. She was in her nightgown, leaning against the bathroom doorframe, watching him shave. Her auburn hair was pulled back in a ponytail, and he'd watched her freckles dance as she talked.

"I'm sure you're going to get the job."

He'd smiled at her, shaving cream still covering half of his face. "Are you now?"

"I know if I was the lieutenant, I'd promote you."

He'd laughed. "I think you're a little biased."

A coy smile had curled at the edge of her lips. "Maaaybe... but you're smart, dedicated, and hard working. What more could he want?"

He'd rinsed his face, accepting the towel she handed him. "Experience, for one. Next to Kevin, I'm the youngest applicant."

"Well, maybe youth is an asset; none of those old habits to break. Besides, you're cuter than all the other applicants."

"Thank you,." he'd bent down and kissed her forehead. "So, if that's the deciding factor, I'm a shoe-in. Is that your position?"

She'd blocked his way out of the bathroom. "It is!"

He'd kissed her again, this time on the lips, then lifted her out of the way. A bright smile lit up her face when he set her down. "And you're strong, too!"

She'd followed him around for the rest of the morning until he left. Cassie knew how important this was to him, and to them. Their baby was due in just a few weeks.

He crossed the squad room and looked into the lieutenant's office. Lieutenant Kelly was on the phone but gestured for Danny to come in and sit down. While he waited and tried to look like he wasn't listening, Danny let his gaze move around the office.

Hung prominently behind the desk, right next to his criminal justice degree, was a commendation from the chief of police. The only photo in the office was sitting on a side table, a five-by-seven of Kelly and his wife on vacation somewhere warm. It might be the most organized office Danny had ever been in.

After less than five minutes, the lieutenant hung up and sat back in his chair, studying the young officer before him. Marcus Kelly had been with the department over twenty years, the last seven spent in charge of Major Case Investigations at the South Boston precinct.

A fit man in his late forties, he had a bright smile and lively eyes, which gave him a friendly aura. His hair had receded halfway back on his head, but a tiny patch of black, barely visible strands, running rearward from just above his forehead gave him a slightly more youthful appearance.

The lieutenant stood, came around the desk, and closed the office door. Instead of returning to his chair, he leaned on the desk, looking down at Danny. "I worked the streets of Southie with your dad, did I ever tell you that?"

Danny's first thought was one he kept to himself.

You may have mentioned a couple dozen times during the interview process.

"Yes, sir."

"I want you to know my decision was not impacted in any way by my relationship with your father."

8

Danny didn't know if that was good or bad. "Yes, sir."

The lieutenant walked back around his desk and opened a drawer. Reaching in, he pulled out a small box, then laid it on Danny's side of the desk. "Congratulations."

Danny didn't move, not sure he'd heard correctly. The lieutenant was smiling at him. "Go ahead; open it."

Danny stood and reached for the box. When he removed the cover, a bronze department badge bearing the designation "Detective" and his name was staring back at him. Danny set the box down and took the badge out. It was attached to a black leather holder that dangled from a silver chain.

Danny brushed the top of the badge with his fingers, feeling like he had when his father had given him a hockey puck autographed by Bobby Orr. It had been priceless to him at the age of ten, and the badge struck him the same way some fifteen years later.

Lieutenant Kelly came around the desk and took it from Danny, then placed it over his head and around his neck. He held out his hand. "Congratulations, Detective Sullivan."

Danny beamed, a silly grin stretching his face. "Thank you, sir. I appreciate it."

A knock came at the office door. The lieutenant went back behind his desk. "Come!"

The door opened and Detective Raymond Murphy came in. Danny recognized him from several of his patrol crime scenes he'd turned over for investigation.

"You wanted to see me, Lieutenant?"

"Yeah, close the door."

Murphy shut the door and cast a sideways glance at Danny. Trying not to look giddy, a difficult task right then, Danny sat back down. He nodded at Murphy, who didn't return the gesture, focusing instead on his boss. "What's up, Lieutenant?"

"I want you to meet your new partner, Danny Sullivan."

Murphy's head swiveled back in Danny's direction, and if he was surprised, he didn't let it show. "Really! Congrats, Sullivan."

Danny stood and shook Murphy's hand. "Thanks."

Murphy looked back at the lieutenant. "Anything else?"

"Nope. You're good to go."

Murphy nodded, opened the door, and left the office. Danny was standing there, unsure of what to do. Lieutenant Kelly pointed at the open door. "Well, go on,

Sullivan. You're his shadow for the foreseeable future."

Danny gathered himself, thanked the lieutenant again, and hurried after Murphy. He caught up with him halfway across the squad room. "Lieutenant Kelly said I should follow you."

"That's right, and you better keep up."

"Yes, sir."

Raymond Murphy stopped in his tracks, almost causing Danny to run into him. "First rule, call me Murph or Murphy, not sir. I'm not your boss, I'm your partner. Clear!"

"Yes, sir... Murph."

"That's your desk."

Danny turned to look at the metal desk with a wood top, scarred by countless previous users. A computer terminal and phone were the only things on it. "Okay"

"I'm right behind you, here." Murph pointed at the desk directly across a small pathway between cubicles.

"Okay," Danny repeated.

"See that board on the wall?"

Danny stared across the room in the direction Murphy indicated. "Yeah."

"That's the open case board. The idea is to *not* have your cases on that board. You want to get them solved and cleared; that's the job. Any questions?"

"No, I don't think so."

"In your top right desk drawer, you'll find a cellphone. It has my number, the lieutenant's number, and the station's number already programmed in it. Don't lose it."

Danny looked over toward the drawer, but before he could say anymore, Murphy was walking away. Danny started to follow him, causing Murphy to call back over his shoulder. "Just going to take a piss. You can follow if you want, but you don't have to."

Danny opted to try out his desk instead.

Sitting down, he noticed the chair was even more worn than the desk. He decided to get his own chair from home. Opening the top drawer, he found the cellphone. A simple black flip-phone, it had obviously been used by detectives before him.

"Congrats, Buddy!"

Danny looked up to see his best friend on the force and former partner, Kevin Doyle.

"Hey, Kevin! Thanks, man." Conflicting emotions swirled through Danny. "I'm glad to get it, but not happy you didn't, you know what I mean?"

"Sure, but if I couldn't get it, I'm glad you're the one who beat me out."

Danny was a year younger than Kevin, but they had entered the academy at the same time, graduated together, and were eventually assigned to the same precinct. They'd ridden together on patrol many times. That part of the job, Danny was going to miss. "I hate that we're not gonna be riding partners again."

Kevin was taller than Danny with thin features and black hair, which despite their shared heritage, made them look like complete opposites. "Did you find out who your partner is?"

"Raymond Murphy."

Kevin nodded. "He's been around, that's for sure."

"Yeah. He'll take some getting used to."

Kevin suddenly appeared uncomfortable and distracted. "Well, I'd better go. I'm due out on patrol in a half hour."

Danny felt the same awkwardness. "Okay. Did *you* get a new partner?"

"Not yet."

"Oh..." Danny let the comment hang in the air.

Kevin nodded and headed out of the squad room.

Danny was surprised at the sadness he felt. Then the phone caught his eye and he realized he hadn't called Cassie. Picking up the receiver, he dialed home.

"Hello?"

"Hey, Cass. It's me."

"And?"   ·

"I got it."

"Yessssssssss!"

The awkwardness of the conversation with Kevin was swept away by his wife's excitement. The grin he wore in the lieutenant's office had returned. "So, you're happy, I guess."

"Very funny! Not only am I happy, I'm proud too."

"Thanks, Cass."

"And I was right!"

Danny laughed. "And yes, you were right."

"Did you call your dad?"

"Not yet."

Her voice softened. "I'll let you go. Call him."

"Okay. I love you."

The line went dead and he punched in his father's number.

"Hello?"

"Hi, Mom. It's Danny."

"I know my boy's voice! How old do you think I am?"

Danny laughed. "How are you doin' today?"

Aileen Sullivan, at fifty-two years young, was the glue that held the Sullivan clan together.

"I'm great, and I still haven't lost my mind, so quit acting like it could happen at any moment!"

"I'm sorry. Is Pop around?"

"Always. Hang on."

There was shuffling as the phone was passed. "Hi, Son."

"Hey, Pop. I got the shield."

There were a few moments of silence, and as always happened when his father choked up, his Irish brogue came through strongly. "Congratulations, Boy. I'm awful proud of you."

Danny nearly cried himself. "Thanks, Pop."

Murphy returned from the bathroom, tapping Danny on the shoulder. "I'm gonna get something to eat across the street."

Danny covered the receiver. "Mind if I tag along?"

"Suit yourself."

Danny uncovered the phone. "Dad, I need to run. Talk to you later?"

"Sure. Bye."

Danny hung up and, for the second time in an hour, chased after Murphy.

****

A block and a half from the precinct was Mul's Diner. On the corner of 'A' Street and West Broadway, just a block and a half from the station, it had the classic embossed-metal diamond front a good diner should have. Black-and-white floor tiles were offset by chrome parlor chairs with red cushions and matching red walls.

Danny followed Murphy to a small booth near the back, where they each ordered coffee and a piece of pie. While they waited, Danny sized up his new partner. Shorter than he was, Murphy had a round face with close-set eyes, and a slightly downturned mouth. Mostly bald, he looked older than his forty-plus years, even though what hair remained was black with no hint of gray.

"What you lookin' at?"

"Nothin'. You mind if I ask you a question?"

"Nope, long as you don't mind me not answering."

"Why didn't you seem surprised when I was dumped on you?"

"You mean 'cause you're new, you're green, and I have to babysit you?"

Danny smiled. "Yeah, something like that."

"Well, 'cause I'm used to it."

"I'm sorry?"

"The lieutenant has used me as a kind of training detective for the last five years. I'm used to it."

The pie and coffees arrived. Danny dumped two cream and two sugars into his cup. "I guess he must trust you, then."

"I never asked him. I just took it as my assignment and did what I was told."

They ate in silence, and after getting a coffee to go, walked back to the precinct.

When they got to their desks, they'd barely set down their coffee cups when Lieutenant Kelly walked by. "I need to see you two in my office."

Danny's first reaction was to wonder what he'd done wrong already.

Murph saw his look. "Time for the first assignment."

Danny smiled. "Oh."

They filed into the lieutenant's office, this time without closing the door, and Kelly held out a sheet of paper to Murphy. "Got a missing persons report this morning. Patrol officer responded and requested a detective. You guys are up."

Murphy took the sheet and turned to go. The lieutenant sat down and turned his attention to some paperwork. Danny was slightly faster on the uptake this time, and followed on Murphy's heels.

Murphy held the sheet behind him for Danny to take. He grabbed it and studied it as they walked to their desks, picked up their coffees, and headed for the car park.

The missing person was a woman named Cary Brennan. She never returned home from work the night before, and was reported missing by her boyfriend. The responding officer was Kevin Doyle.

Danny's heart began to pound. He was on his first case.

BRENNAN RESIDENCE
SOUTH BOSTON
12:00 P.M.

They arrived at the address on East 5th just past noon. A two-story row house, newly remodeled with gray siding and upgraded windows, it was one of a half-dozen on the block.

Murphy parked the car across the street and got out. "I'll ask the questions initially. You take notes and check out the surroundings. Make sure to write down anything you think is odd or out of place. If you have a question to ask, wait until I look at you and walk away."

"Why wait until you walk away?"

"That will give me a chance to look for things that I think are out of the ordinary. We can compare notes when the interview is over."

"Got it."

They crossed to the front entrance and rang the bell. After just a minute or so, the door swung open. A man in his early forties, plain but clean cut, stood in the opening. "Yes?"

Murphy flashed his badge. "Detective Murphy with the Boston PD. This is my partner, Detective Sullivan."

Danny nodded but didn't say anything. The man stepped aside and cleared the way for the detectives. "My name is Joe Turner. Please, come in."

Murphy went in, followed by Danny, and they waited while Mr. Turner closed the door. They found themselves in a long hallway with a handful of doorways on either side, and they could see the kitchen at the far end. Frank gestured toward the first doorway on the left, which led into a sitting parlor. "We can talk in here."

Danny leaned against the doorframe while Murphy sat in a chair across the coffee table from Joe Turner. Murphy took out his notebook. "Any word from Miss Brennan since you spoke with the officer earlier?"

"No, nothing."

"And your connection to her is?"

"I'm her boyfriend. We live here together."

Danny had his own pad out, but he was only listening vaguely. His eyes traveled around the room, looking for any sign of a struggle, or anything out of place. There was nothing obvious, so he leaned back, looking down the hallway toward the kitchen. From his vantage point, the kitchen looked to be in order. In fact, the house was neatly kept and appeared in good condition.

Murphy was still getting the basics. "When was the last time you saw Miss Brennan?"

"Yesterday afternoon, when she left for work."

"What time was that?"

"Around two. She works a three-to-midnight shift at Boston Medical Center."

"Did you talk to her while she was at work?"

Turner sat on the edge of the couch, rubbing his hands together nervously. "Yeah. She always calls me when she learns when she will get off. Sometimes she has to work overtime."

"And did she expect to get off on time last night?"

"Yeah."

"What time was that call?"

Turner picked up his phone, pushed a few buttons, then held it out for the detective. "Eleven thirty-eight."

"And what time would she normally arrive home?"

"About twelve thirty."

Danny was watching Murphy closer than Turner. Gaining important information through questioning was as much art as science, and Murphy had been doing it a long time. Danny found it fascinating.

Murphy kept the tone of his voice flat and his face expressionless. He'd jot the answer down to a question before moving on. More importantly, Murphy's stare would return to Turner's face before he would ask the next question. "Did you talk to anyone at her work?"

"Yes. They said she left on time."

"Who did you talk to?"

"Her supervisor."

"What's her supervisor's name?"

"Carol Nelson in pediatrics."

Murphy hesitated before asking his next question, his voice staying flat, but the question delivered at a slower pace. He was watching Turner's reaction. "Why... did you wait... until almost noon to report her... missing?"

Turner's head dropped slightly, and his eyes shifted from Murphy's stare. "I... well... I fell asleep. I didn't even know she wasn't home until nearly ten."

Murphy now looked down at his notes, but didn't write anything. Quite suddenly, he lifted his head and leaned in slightly toward Turner. "How is your relationship with Miss Brennan?"

Turner literally slid back on couch, trying to restore the distance between him and the detective. "Good. I mean... we have our spats like anyone... but good."

Murphy was still leaning forward. "What about yesterday, any arguments?"

Turner started to stammer. "No... Well, yeah... I mean it was no big deal."

"What exactly was it about?"

"Money. I don't have a job right now and she was a little angry about it."

"She wants you to find work sooner rather than later."

"Something like that, but like I said, it was no big deal."

Murphy turned and looked at Danny. "Maybe it was to her."

There was a moment of tense silence, then Murphy stood. "Do you mind if we have a look around, Mr. Turner?"

"No... go ahead."

Danny took his cue and moved into the room. A photo of a woman sat on the mantle. "Is this Miss Brennan?"

Turner looked up at him as if he'd forgotten Danny was there. "Uh... yeah, that's from a New Year's party last year."

Danny picked up the photo and studied it. Cary Brennan, who Danny already knew was forty-three, had dirty-blonde hair and brown, expressive eyes. Her smile was wide and her teeth perfect. "She's a pretty lady."

Turner nodded. "Very."

"Does she have any identifying marks, a birthmark or tattoo for instance?"

"Yeah. She went to Boston College. She has a flying eagle above one ankle and BC above the other."

Danny made a note of the tattoos. "Can we have this photo?"

"Sure. You'll give it back when you find her?"

"Of course." Danny took Murphy's place in the chair across from Turner, who had left the room to look around. "Does she have any family?"

"No. This house belonged to her mother, who passed away. Her father died years ago. She was an only child."

"What kind of car does she drive?"

"She doesn't have a car. She takes the bus."

"Do you have any idea where she might have gone?"

"That's the thing, she always comes home after work. She's too exhausted to do much else after a shift."

"What about any enemies? Is there anyone she's had a disagreement with?"

Turner shook his head. "Nothing out of the ordinary, other than the Peeping Tom reports last month."

Danny stared at Turner. "Peeping Tom reports?"

"Yeah. Some guy was looking through the kitchen window. She called you guys."

"Did they catch him?"

"No, he was long gone. They took a report and that was the last we heard of it."

"Did you get a good look at him?"

"I wasn't home the second time. Cary gave them a description, but she didn't see much."

"The second time?"

"Yeah, it happened twice. First time, I came home right after she saw him. I went outside, but he was gone. We reported it and an officer took down the information."

"And the second instance?"

"Like I said, I wasn't here, but they sent out a detective. We didn't hear anything about either of them again."

Murphy came back into the room, and Danny stood to let Murphy have his seat, but instead his partner gestured for them to leave. "Mr. Turner, we've got enough for now." He pulled out a business card and handed it to the man. "If you think of anything else, or hear from her, please call me immediately."

Turner stared at the card. "I will."

Thirty seconds later, they were outside and back in the car. Murphy started it and pulled into traffic. "Did you learn anything?"

"Yeah. Your questioning tactics were very interesting."

Murphy grinned at him. "Not about that! Did you learn anything more about our case while I was out of the room?"

Danny was sure he blushed. "Oh, yeah. Cary Brennan reported a Peeping Tom twice last month."

"Oh?"

"Yeah, Turner said she filed a report both times, but didn't get a good look at him."

"We need to pull those reports."

"Okay. Also, Miss Brennan doesn't own a vehicle. She takes the bus to and from work."

"I know."

Danny looked up in surprise. He didn't remember Murphy asking about transportation. "How?"

"Expired bus pass in the bedroom."

Danny nodded. "Did you see anything else?"

"Nothing. The stuff you would expect to be gone if somebody packed up is all still there, and if something bad happened to her, it didn't look like it was there. What about you? Did you see anything out of the ordinary?"

"No, but I did snag this photo of our missing girl."

Murphy glanced at it. "Pretty lady."

"That's what I said."

BOSTON MEDICAL CENTER
SOUTH BOSTON
3:00 P.M.

Fighting their way through traffic, they finally arrived at Boston Medical Center. The City of Boston is consistently listed in the top five or six of the worst traffic spots in the nation, and with the on-going growth, it wasn't going to improve any time soon.

Murphy parked in the Official Vehicles Only area and they walked in through the emergency entrance. Boston Medical Center was a teaching hospital with roughly five hundred beds and over a million patients a year. It was like walking inside a beehive: unending sound and constant motion.

Since it was past time for Cary Brennan's shift to begin, the two detectives took the elevator directly to the pediatrics floor. When they stepped off, a large semi-circle desk that served as the nurse's station, was directly in front of them. Danny followed Murphy, who waved at a young woman in white. "Janet! Nice to see ya. I'm looking for Carol Nelson."

"She's in her office. Take the corridor, second door on the left."

"Thanks." They found it easily, and the woman sitting at the desk gestured them in while she finished her phone call. They each took a chair and waited.

Carol Nelson appeared to Danny to be in her mid-fifties, with gray hair pulled in a tight bun and pinned beneath a white nurse's cap. She had a deep voice that carried an air of authority, especially when she was aggravated, which sounded like the case just then. Her face showed the crags of stress and her eyes appeared tired beyond their years. It was nearly ten minutes before she got off the phone. "I'm so sorry. That was unavoidable, I'm afraid. How can I help you?"

"My name is Detective Murphy, and this is my partner, Detective Sullivan. We're looking into the disappearance of Cary Brennan, one of your nurses."

"Disappearance?"

"Yes. Her boyfriend reported her missing."

"I spoke to Joe this morning. He said he was worried about her but I didn't know it was that serious."

"I gather she hasn't shown up for her shift today?"

"She didn't call in to me. Let me check."

The head nurse left and returned in less than two minutes. "Nobody has seen her, and she didn't call in."

Danny took out his notepad as Murphy quizzed Miss Nelson. "Has she ever done this before?"

The nurse shook her head. "Cary is one of my best nurses, both in quality of care and reliability. She is always here when she's scheduled."

"What about Joe Turner? Did she mention any problems at home?"

"No. Not to me, anyway."

"What about here at work? Is there anyone she's had a run-in with?"

Carol Nelson shook her head emphatically. "Definitely not. Cary got along with everyone."

Murphy pulled out a business card and slid it across the desk. "If you think of anything or hear from Miss Brennan, please call us immediately."

"Of course."

Murphy stood and Danny followed suit. They said their goodbyes and headed out of the office. Danny pushed the button to call the elevator. "Where to now?"

"Security."

"Oh, okay. Why?"

The doors slid open and they stepped in. "I want to make sure our girl got on her regular bus."

****

The security office was on the ground floor, not far from the main entrance. A young man with red hair and nervous eyes was at the desk. The bank of screens from multiple security cameras flashed off his face as he looked up. "Can I help you?"

29

Murphy flashed his badge. "Detective Murphy, Boston PD. This is my partner, Detective Sullivan."

Danny liked the sound of his name attached to "detective" and was already starting to get used to it. He exposed his badge for the security guy.

Murphy moved around the desk so he could look at the video screens. "We're investigating a missing persons case involving one of your employees. Her name is Cary Brennan. Sound familiar?"

The guard shook his head. "No, sorry. There's over five thousand employees in this place."

Murphy smiled. "Yeah, I didn't imagine you had all the names memorized." He pointed at one particular screen. "That camera there, can we see the tape from it?"

"What time frame? These are all on forty-eight hour loops."

"Last night, say starting from midnight."

"Sure."

The guard punched several buttons and pretty soon the current daylight shot changed to darkness. The camera Murphy had chosen showed the front walk leading out to the bus stop. The loop began at eleven-fifty five, and after watching a fast playback for less than a minute, their missing girl came into the frame, walking down the front steps.

Danny pointed. "That's her!"

The guard stopped the tape, but Murphy tapped his shoulder. "Let it run."

At regular speed, they watched her get to the bus stop, wait several minutes, then get on. She never saw or talked to anyone. Murphy made a note of the time she got on the bus, then thanked the guard. "Oh, can we get a copy of that?"

"I suppose."

"Good. Have it sent over to the 6th precinct on Broadway, attention Detective Murphy."

"No problem."

"Thanks again."

They left the office and Danny fell in step with his partner. "Where to now?"

"Back to the precinct. We need to get a BOLO put out and run the boyfriend's name for a record."

Danny was pretty sure *"We"* probably meant *"He"* needed put out a be-on-lookout and run a records check.

PRECINCT C-6
5:10 P.M.

When they came back into the squad room, several other detectives were gathered at the open case board. They turned as Murphy and his young protégé walked by. One of the older detectives, bald and round, laughed. "Hey, Murph! Got ya another greenhorn, huh?"

Murphy didn't stop. "That's right! They want me to get him ready for your retirement."

Baldy's smile disappeared. "I ain't retiring!"

"Not voluntarily, you mean?"

Baldy now looked at the other detectives, then back at Murphy. "You know something I don't, Murph?"

"Yeah... You're a gullible chump!"

The group started laughing at the old detective. Baldy just sneered. "Very funny!"

Danny dropped into his desk chair and turned on his computer. As he sat there doing the record search on the boyfriend, each detective came by and patted his shoulder.

"Welcome, Sullivan."

Except Baldy.

Eventually, Murphy stood up. "Did you run the BOLO?"

"Not yet. Have it done in a few."

"Good. I had the phone company ping our missing lady's phone but it came up empty. Either it's dead or off. Run the BOLO, then call it a day. I'll see you in the morning."

"Okay. Goodnight."

Twenty minutes later, Danny's personal cellphone rang. "Hello?"

"Danny?"

"Yes. Who did you expect?"

Cassie laughed. "I'm not sure. When will you be home?"

Danny looked at his computer screen. It was already past six. "I should be leaving here soon."

"Good, because everyone is here."

"What do you mean?"

"Your mom, dad, and granddad... everyone."

"Why?"

"Why do you think, dummy? We're celebrating."

It hadn't occurred to him they'd have a party. "Oh."

"Just get here as soon as you can, okay?"

"I will."

He hung up and went to retrieve the print-off of Frank Turner's file. It was nice they wanted to celebrate his promotion, but right then, he was more tired than excited.

SULLIVAN RESIDENCE
WEST ROXBURY
6:45 P.M.

Home for Danny and Cass was in West Roxbury, a neighborhood in the southwest section of the city. Tree-lined streets with single-family homes dating back as far as the 1850s were the rule, and many civil servants like Danny lived there. The large Irish community made them feel right at home.

Both Danny and Cass would prefer to live in Southie, closer to his work and all the amenities, but the price of homes in that area had far exceeded a policeman's salary. Still, the drive to the station was less than ten miles, which in Boston time was roughly thirty minutes on a good day.

Danny parked by the curb in front of the single-story bungalow on Dent Street. Brick steps led up to the door with large picture windows on either side. White clapboard siding was dressed up with blue shutters. It was small but they loved the backyard, which was fenced and stretched far enough to accommodate touch-football games.

As he came through the front door, a cheer went up. "He's here! Let's eat!"

Danny laughed as his mother wrapped him in a big hug. "Congratulations, Danny."

She looked good, her light red hair swept up, and her lips covered with her trademark red lipstick. At fifty-two, she was the backbone of the family, making sure no one forgot what was most important: each other.

"Thanks, Mom."

His father was right behind her, and his patent ironworker handshake was a reward in itself. Danny had always known he'd done well if his father shook his hand with that certain extra. "Congratulations, Son."

Pat Sullivan had been a Boston cop for fifteen years, making shift-sergeant, but his career came to an end when a bullet during a convenience store robbery lodged in his hip. That was ten years ago and the limp had grown worse lately. "Thanks, Pop. It means alot coming from you."

Cass came out of the kitchen carrying a large cast-iron pot filled with Irish stew. It was one of Danny's favorites. Lamb shoulder with celery, carrots, onions, and potatoes. "Hey, honey. Are you hungry?"

"Famished."

"Well, get cleaned up and come to the table."

Danny went down the short hallway to their bedroom. He laid his gun, new badge, cuffs, and various other pieces of the daily uniform, on the dresser. Going into the bathroom, he splashed water on his face.

When he returned to the table, stew was already in bowls. He bent over and kissed Cass on the cheek before sitting down at the head of the table. His father said grace, and everyone attacked their food.

Sitting at the opposite end of the table was his grandfather, Francis Sullivan. Now seventy-four, he too had walked a beat for the department. He'd retired a lieutenant, having served the same area of South Boston for thirty-three years. "Hi, Grandad."

His grandfather, mouth already full of stew, nodded.

Cass reserved two pieces of garlic soda bread for Danny, then passed it around. Forty-five minutes later, there was hardly a scrap of food left over.

Danny got up from the table and went into the living room. Already sitting in the worn armchair was his grandfather, a cup of coffee spiked with just a touch of whiskey, resting on his lap. He smiled up at his grandson. "Big day, huh?"

Danny smiled, carrying his own cup of coffee, minus the whiskey. "Yeah."

"I understand you already have your first case."

Danny nodded, sipping his coffee. "Missing woman."

Frank sipped his own coffee, apparently not interested in any details. Unexpectedly, Danny's curiosity about his grandfather's career was piqued.

They'd talked many times, when Danny was younger, about life on the force and particular incidents that occurred while his grandfather was with the Boston PD. Very few of those conversations were about the private side of things. "Can I ask you a personal question?"

"Of course."

"Was Grandmother ever disappointed you didn't make detective?"

The elderly man set his coffee cup on the side table and removed his oversized turtle-shell glasses. He put one arm of the spectacles in his mouth, a pose Danny was familiar with. He'd seen it all his life when his grandfather was serious about a question, whether it was answering one or asking one. "You know, she never said."

Danny's grandmother had passed away nearly eight years ago, enjoying just a short time of Frank's retirement. It was a devastating blow to the whole family, and everyone grieved for a long time. Danny hadn't been sure his grandfather would ever come around.

Eventually, the grit that had made him a good cop pulled him through. Frank was smiling at Danny, his glasses having returned to his face. "Toughest job in the world."

Danny was confused. "Being a detective?"

His grandfather chuckled. "No. Being a cop's wife."

Danny nodded, looking through the kitchen door to where Cass and his mother were doing the dishes. "Yeah, I imagine. I think Cass worries all the time."

"So did your grandmother. She dealt with it by using her rosary; seemed like she wore one out every couple months."

Danny laughed as his phone rang. Looking at the number, he pushed answer. "Hey, Sean."

"Hey, yourself. Congrats, Bro!"

Sean was Danny's younger brother. Just two years Danny's junior, he was in his final year of police academy. "Thanks. How did you find out?"

Sean grunted. "Do you really have to ask?"

Danny laughed. It would be their mother. "No, I guess not."

"Had to beat me to it, didn't ya?"

"No doubt. I've whipped your butt all your life, no sense stopping now!"

"Whatever. You get a partner?"

"Yeah, his name is Raymond Murphy."

"You like him?"

"Seems okay, so far."

"Good. I gotta run, but I'll see you at Thanksgiving."

"Okay, bye."

As soon as he hung up, a text message came through.

Congrats, big brother!

He smiled as he typed his response. 'Thanks, Sis. Mom call you?'

Of course! Left me a message during calculus after I had to silence my phone!

His sister was away at Bridgewater State University, in the southern part of the state, getting her teaching degree. At twenty-one, she was the baby of the family. Danny missed his sister being around. 'See you at Thanksgiving?'

You bet! Touch-football in the backyard?

'Definitely. Miss you, Sis.'

Same here. Congrats again.

****

A couple hours later, Danny locked up the house and headed for the bedroom. Cass was already under the covers, doing her best not to be miserable. He couldn't imagine walking and sleeping with a beach ball, weighing as much as two gallons of milk, attached to his stomach.

Despite his exhaustion, he sat down on her side of the bed and rubbed her hair. "Has the baby been active?"

"Non-stop. Perhaps you could talk to her, tell her it's time to come out."

He smiled. "Her? You mean him, don't you?"

"I don't know, but the way this baby kicks, you may be right."

"How's your back?"

"Sore."

"You didn't have to make the stew. I'd have been glad to bring something home."

She rolled her eyes. "You don't think I made it, do you? Your mother showed up with stew and bread in hand. I just had to keep it warm until you got here."

Danny laughed. "I should have known."

He stood, kissed her forehead, and went into the bathroom. After washing up, he returned to the bed and was about to climb in when he remembered. Going to the dresser, he picked up the precinct cellphone and laid it on the table next to the bed. Five minutes later, he was out cold.

BOSTON HOMICIDE

.

42

TUESDAY, NOVEMBER 2

SULLIVAN RESIDENCE
WEST ROXBURY
3:45 A.M.

Danny wasn't sure why he was being rocked back and forth like he was on a boat, but soon realized it was Cass trying to wake him. "Danny! Your phone."

He pawed at his eyes, trying to force them open and bring himself around. "What?"

"The precinct phone was going off."

Danny rolled on his side and picked up the cellphone. When he flipped it open, Murphy's number was lit up as a missed call. Before he could call back, it started to ring again. "Hello?"

"Danny?"

"Yeah, Murph. It's early, what's up?"

"I know what time it is. You need to get up."

Danny looked at the bedside clock. "Why?"

"A patrol unit has found a body and they think it matches our BOLO."

Danny's heart rate picked up and he found himself instantly moving. "Really! Where?"

"Behind the Calf Pasture Pump Station. You know it?"

"Sure, near the Kennedy Library."

"That's the place. Meet me there as soon as you can."

"On my way."

CALF PASTURE II
DORCHESTER
4:20 A.M.

One good thing about being up at that hour was the light traffic. It took him less than twenty minutes from the time he left the house. The Calf Pasture was a park had got the name from its former use. Now it was part of the Harborwalk and the revamped waterfront.

Coming down Mount Vernon Street, it was easy to find the scene as he approached the pump station. Red and blue lights bounced off the trees and buildings, giving the appearance a macabre circus had come to town. Danny parked at the edge of the crime tape and walked toward the officer on watch.

He recognized Jack Duffy, a patrolman from the precinct. "Hey, Jack. You the one who found the girl?"

"Yeah, it's not pretty. I was making my rounds, and when I made a loop through this lot, my lights swept across her. What are you doing up at this hour?"

Danny pulled his badge from under his jacket. Jack's eyebrows went up. "I hadn't heard."

"Just happened yesterday. Is Murphy here?"

Jack lifted the tape and pointed at the collection of people about fifty yards away. "He's over there."

"Thanks."

"By the way, congrats."

"I appreciate it."

Danny approached the group, most wearing city coroner or crime scene investigator jackets. Photo flashes added to the chaos, and Danny kept his distance until he'd circled around the group and found Murphy. "Hey, Murph. I got here as quick as I could."

Murphy nodded and stepped back. "I just got here myself."

"Is it our girl?"

"See for yourself."

Danny moved forward until he could see the body. Laying on a small rise beneath the trees was a nude female. Danny looked at the face and his blood ran cold. Whoever she was, her facial features were not going to be of any use in identifying her. "Dear God, she's a mess."

"Yeah. No ID or personal belongings have been found."

Danny took in the rest of the scene. She was lying on her back, her legs spread apart, and her arms splayed out from her sides as if she was doing some sort of repugnant snow angel. Other than the head, the rest of the body seemed to have very little trauma to it. "Why did they think this was our girl?"

"Look at the ankles."

Danny bent over and caught sight of the flying eagle tattoo. On the other ankle was the matching BC ink, making it almost a certainty this was Cary Brennan. "Do they have a cause of death, other than the obvious trauma to the head?"

"Not officially. They'll wait until autopsy."

Danny let his gaze take in the entire area. Officers with flashlights were moving slowly around the perimeter of the crime scene. It was secluded, but accessible from the nearby parking lot. A voice called out from the darkness. "Detectives!"

The two investigators went over to where the officer was standing and he

shined his flashlight on a depression in the dirt. "Looks like it might be where he dumped the body out of the car," He let the flashlight play along the dirt in the direction of the body. "There's drag marks from here until you hit the grass."
Murphy hunched down, his own flashlight shining slightly to the side of the drag marks. A clear footprint was visible in the dirt. Murphy stood up. "Brody! You got a minute?"

The photographer, who had stopped taking pictures and was messing with his camera, came over. "What's up, Murph?"

"Got a footprint here. I'd like it photographed, then casted."

Brody examined the print illuminated by Murphy's light. "Nice one. Okay, I'll take care of it."

Murphy turned to the officer who had called them over. "Run some more tape around this and keep everyone away."

"Yes, sir."

The two detectives walked back over to where the body was, and watched the coroner work.

Doctor Megan Quinn was in her late thirties and had started as a morgue assistant, working through college, and had eventually made her way up to district coroner. Her dark brown hair was perpetually in a ponytail, and very little makeup ever found its way onto her face.

While not unattractive, Megan's beauty was in her brains, and she was very good at what she did. Right then, she was examining the wrists of their victim. "Restraints were used, probably zip-ties."

Murphy took out his notepad and scribbled it down. "Ankles, too?"

"Don't think so."

"Any estimate on time of death, Megan?"

"Over twenty-four hours, but that's as close as I would want to guess right now."

More scribbling from Murphy. "Lack of blood seems to indicate she was killed somewhere else and dumped."

The coroner smiled up at Murphy. "Very good, Murph. Pretty soon you won't need me on your cases."

Murphy put away his notepad. "We all know you're irreplaceable, Doc."

Megan Quinn rolled her eyes. "Said the detective who's untouchable!"

Murphy laughed as he turned and headed for his car. The sun was just making its way over the horizon as Danny fell in stride. "What does she mean by 'untouchable'?"

"She likes to give me a hard time. I've had a few scrapes with Internal Affairs but nothing came of it."

"What kind of scrapes?"

Murphy climbed into his car and cast a sideways glance up at his young partner. "Don't worry, you haven't been entrusted to a dirty cop."

"No... I didn't mean..."

Murphy grinned at him. "Take it easy, I'm just jerking your chain. Meet me at the station."

"Yeah, okay."

BRENNAN RESIDENCE
SOUTH BOSTON
6:55 A.M.

After getting into Murphy's car, they headed to Cary Brennan's home. Murphy had already checked to see if Joe Turner was there, and told him they would be coming by.

Danny had never done a death notification before, but he could sense the tension in his partner, and found himself dreading it also.

49

Murphy rang the bell and Turner answered the door almost before the bell had fallen silent. Danny instantly spotted the fear in the man's eyes. "Morning, detectives."

Murphy nodded. "Mind if we come in?"

Turner stood aside and let them in. "Of course."

All three returned to the parlor they'd been sitting in less than twenty-four hours earlier. Murphy sat, and Joe lowered himself slowly opposite the detective. He took a quick glance at Danny, then met the gaze of Murphy. "Did you get a lead on Cary?"

Murphy hesitated briefly. "Yeah... We found her."

"And? Is she okay?"

"I'm sorry to have to tell you this, but Miss Brennan was murdered."

"Murdered?"

"I'm afraid so."

Turner dropped his face into his hands. His sobbing filled the room while Danny and Murph exchanged glances. Murphy waited until the man composed himself before delivering the next piece of news. "We need you to look at a couple photos to make a positive ID. It won't be a pleasant task."

"How did she die?"

"We're not certain yet, but she suffered a severe beating."

The man's eyes were red but Danny was unsure if he saw tears. "Do you have the photos with you?"

Danny handed the file folder he was carrying to Murph, who put it on the table. "When you're ready, open the folder."

Turner looked at it, then at Murphy. His hand shook as he reached toward the pictures. The first photo was of the eagle, and elicited a moan from Joe. He slid it out of the way and looked at the second one, the BC tattoo. "Oh, Cary..."

Turner paused before looking at the third photo. When he saw it, he eyes closed and he turned away. Danny thought the man might throw-up when he covered his mouth.

"I understand," Murphy closed the folder. "I take it you're sure?"

Turner nodded, his eyes still closed. "Do you have any suspects?"

"I'm afraid I can't discuss that right now."

The answer was no, but Danny could sense Murph was sizing up Turner and his reaction. Every first-day academy cadet knew it was usually the boyfriend or the husband, but Danny had to caution himself. *Unless it's not.*

Joe Turner stood. "I need a drink."

Murphy stood with him. "I'd prefer you didn't. We need to ask you a few questions."

"Of water, Detective."

"Oh, of course."

When Joe left the room, Murph looked at Danny with a half-grin. "That's not what I would have wanted to drink just then."

Turner came back in with a glass. "I'm ready; let's get this over with."

While Turner sat back down, both detectives pulled out their notepads. Danny handled the generic questions first. "Does Miss Brennan have any relatives that need to be notified?"

Turner shook his head. "She inherited this house from her mom, who passed away over a year ago. She has an ex-husband, but they've been divorced more than ten years."

"What's his name?"

"Alex Brennan."

"Do you know where he lives?"

"San Francisco, last I heard."

"Do you know why they divorced?"

Turner nodded. "He decided he was gay."

Danny jotted down the info, but had already mentally ruled out the ex. They would still need to check it out, though.

Murphy now got to the more delicate, and important questions. "You said you fell asleep the night Miss Brennan went missing, do you know what time it was?"

"The last time I remember looking at the clock was one-thirty."

"And you weren't concerned then?"

"Sure, a little, but I figured the busses were slow or something."

"And what time did you wake up?"

"Around ten the next morning."

Murphy's flat tone from the day before was gone. He sounded much more suspicious now. "You were awfully tired, weren't you?"

Turner stared into his glass, avoiding Murphy's eyes. "Yeah... Well, I'd had a couple drinks."

Danny was growing uncomfortable with the mood and felt Murphy may be crossing the line. After all they'd just told Joe his girlfriend was dead.

Murphy didn't let up. "Just a couple?"

Turner had heard enough. "Yeah! Just a couple." The man looked at Danny for some help. "Is this really necessary right now?"

Murphy abruptly stood, gathered up the folder, and moved to the door. "That's all we need at the moment. Don't leave town."

Turner didn't get another word out before the two detectives had walked outside. On the way to the car, Danny spoke his mind. "You were pretty hard on him, weren't you, Murph?"

Murphy stopped and turned to his partner. "It's a little soon to be questioning my methods, isn't it, Sullivan?"

Danny began to backpedal. "Well... I don't mean..."

Murphy started walking again. "Look, I know it seemed harsh, but that was the moment to get the best information possible from him. He was off-balance from doing the ID, and lying to us was going to be difficult."

"Makes sense, I guess."

Murphy looked across the top of the car before getting in. "I know how it looked, and I don't really like doing it, but our job is to find out who killed his loved one. If ruffling his feathers a little accomplishes that, so be it."

Danny had to admit his partner was right, but it didn't make him feel any better. He got into the car and out of the chilly morning wind. A frigid wind made worse by the cold-blooded murder of an innocent woman.

MBTA HEADQUARTERS, DOWNTOWN BOSTON 9:20 A.M.

Most, but not all, of the busses and trains in the Massachusetts Bay Transportation system have cameras. Some have hard drives that have to be retrieved, but some have an automatic feed from the bus to the transit central headquarters. When Danny called to inquire if the route Cary Brennan rode had cameras with direct feeds, they struck gold.

They parked in the public lot off of Charles Street and made their way to the elevators. Murphy had been mostly quiet since leaving Joe Turner, and Danny had not pushed his luck. He was happy to ride in silence.

The elevator doors opened on the third floor and they quickly found the MBTA office. A pleasant-looking lady, whose eyes revealed an already difficult day, tried to smile as they entered.

Murphy flashed his badge. "Detective Murphy, Boston PD. We need to speak with Larry Cornell."

"Very well, I'll let him know."

She picked up the phone while Murphy stared at her. Danny had taken a chair next to a pile of magazines. The cramped waiting area was meant to discourage waiting. The receptionist put the phone down. "He'll be up in a minute."

Murphy flashed a smile. "Thanks."

Less than a minute later, the side door opened and a round man in his mid-forties, wearing an MBTA shirt that appeared one size too small, peered around the doorframe. "Detective Murphy?"

Murphy held his hand up, even though there wasn't anyone else in the room besides Danny. "Here!"

"Come with me."

Murphy held the door for Danny, and they followed the man down a short hallway into an office. The morning sun came in through large windows and removed the need for any heat. Murphy took the chair offered. "This is my partner, Detective Sullivan."

The man shook both the detectives' hands. "Larry Cornell. I took the liberty of calling up the video you were asking about."

Cornell moved around and sat behind his desk, then turned the computer monitor toward the detectives. "The section I've cued up goes from midnight on the day you requested and starts just as the bus pulls up at the medical center."

Danny stepped closer, peering over Murphy's shoulder, as the images started to move. The bus stopped and the driver swung the door open, then greeted the lone figure stepping on. It was Cary Brennan. They watched until the bus reached Andrew Station. Cornell stopped the tape. "I then pulled the video from her connection and found this."

The second video showed Cary Brennan on the connecting bus alone except for the driver. After ten minutes, she climbed off and the bus moved on. Larry stopped the tape. "I counted the stops and she got off at 4th and N Street."

Murphy stood and looked at Danny. "Well, that's her stop. Whatever happened to her took place between there and home."

Murphy thanked Cornell and requested copies. In the elevator, Danny asked an obvious question. "Now what?"

Murphy stared at him. "What would you do?"

Danny thought about it for a minute, long enough for the elevator doors to open. He hadn't come up with anything and so continued to think about it until they were back at the car. Murphy stopped and looked across the top, something that Danny was starting to realize was a habit. "Well, what did you come up with?"

"If it was me, I'd want to know if anybody along her walking route saw anything that night."

"Well, it is you, and that's a good idea. Let's go."

BUS STOP, 4TH & N SOUTH BOSTON 10:30 A.M.

Murphy found a space on N Street, just up from the bus stop. They walked to the stop and planned their route. Murphy was pointing. "Straight down N to Fifth, then half a block over is the most direct and likely route."

"Makes sense. You want one side of the street and I'll take the other?"

"Nah, let's work together. Sometimes people are quicker to dismiss a lone detective than a pair."

"Okay with me. Let's go."

There were no less than twenty duplex and multi-family units between the stop and the Brennan home. By lunch, they'd hit less than half. Murphy came down the walk from ringing the bell at the third house with no one home. "You getting hungry?"

"Yeah."

"There's a little place called the Sidewalk Cafe on the next block."

Danny had seen it. "Yeah, I've driven by on patrol."

"Let's get some food and we'll start back up after lunch."

"Sounds like a plan."

As they walked toward the restaurant, Murphy looked at his notes. "Nothing from the people we've talked to, and five places with nobody home. We'll need to hit those later."

Danny wondered if "later" was that afternoon or that night, but he didn't ask.

****

After lunch and several cups of coffee, they resumed their neighborhood canvas. By three in the afternoon, they had made the turn onto 5th Street and were working toward the Brennan place.

Six more houses had been added to the list of "not home," and Murphy was getting impatient. "Okay, I think you know what we're after. We'll be here all night if we don't get moving. You take that side and I'll take this one."

Danny was more than ready to get this done, especially because nothing had come of it so far. "Works for me."

Two hours later, the first run of the canvas was done. Seven homes had been added to the "not home" list. Danny was exhausted and Murphy didn't look much better. "You get anything, Murph?"

"Nothing."

"How many not-home addresses?"

"Eighteen."

They started walking back to the car. Danny didn't want to ask the next question, but he was too tired to stop himself. "When do we re-check them?"

"Tonight, after dinner."

"I was afraid you'd say that."

Murphy laughed. "You weren't *afraid*. You *knew* I was going to say that."

Danny had to laugh. "True fact!"

"When we get back to the station, go home and have dinner with Cassie, then meet me here at seven-thirty."

"Seven-thirty, it is."

It was actually seven-forty-five when Danny found Murphy parked in the same spot. He had planned to be on time, but Cass was not happy about him going back out so late. He'd done his best to make her understand that this was the way it was as a detective, but she was nine months pregnant, and expecting her to be agreeable may have been a little too optimistic on his part.

The wind had picked up after dark, and Danny hurried to jump into Murphy's car. His partner didn't mention the time. "Okay, I've divided these in half." He tore a piece of paper out of his pad. "Here's yours, and I've got mine. Keep going until you find something or you've crossed everyone off."

Danny nodded. "Let's go."

Going down N Street was the same as it was during the afternoon, except he'd found someone home at each of his addresses, but still no one who'd seen or heard anything early that Monday morning. He reached the last house on his side of N, and rang the bell. A man in his late-twenties answered. "Yeah?"

"Good evening. My name is Detective Sullivan with Boston PD." Danny showed his badge. "Mind if I ask you a couple questions?"

The young man brushed his blond hair out of his eyes. "No sweat. Come in, man."

Danny stepped inside the door, and thought he may have caught a whiff of something illegal. But that wasn't what he was there for. "What's your name?"

"Greg... Greg Larson."

Danny pulled out a picture of Cary Brennan. "Have you ever seen this lady?"

Greg peered at it. "No... I don't think so. Why?"

Danny was tired and not pulling any punches. "She was murdered Monday morning."

"Murdered? Dude, that's awful."

"Indeed. Did you happen to see anything unusual after midnight Sunday, into the early hours of Monday?"

"Unusual? No man."

This guy was wearing on Danny's patience. "What about a car or stranger in the area?"

"Nah... Not that I remember."

Danny doubted Greg could remember what he had for lunch. "Okay, I appreciate your time." He turned to leave.

"Well, you know what?"

Danny stopped.

"I was in the bathroom late one night, I think it was Sunday, and heard some talking."

Danny's pulse quickened. "Oh?"

"Yeah, I had to piss... Alot of beer that night, you know?"

"Sure."

"Anyway, I'm standing there doin' my business when I heard these voices. I pulled back the blind and saw a car. The guy inside was talkin' to some chick who was bundled up."

Danny had his notepad out. "Can you describe the car?"

"Nah, man. I just looked then let the blind drop. It was gray, that's all I saw."

"Big car, little car?"

"Umm... big. You know, like a sedan."

"Did you get a look at the man or the woman?"

"Nah, dude. Like I said, it was real fast."

"Okay, Greg. I'm gonna leave you my partner's card, and ask you to call if you think of anything else, okay?"

Greg appeared to be quite proud of himself, a silly grin spreading across his face. "Sure, no problem."

Danny stepped out into the cold again, looking for Murph. He found him finishing up the last house on Fifth. "I may have got something."

"Well, that's one of us! What is it?"

Danny recounted the interview with Greg Larson. Murphy seemed less than inspired. "Well, that's something, although it's almost impossible to do a search for a gray sedan."

Danny was a little deflated. "I guess."

"Hey, I said *almost* impossible. Good work, rookie. It's been a long day and the autopsy is scheduled for eight in the morning. Let's go home."

Danny looked at the time on his phone. Ten-fifteen. Cass might still be up because she was so uncomfortable, but if she was asleep, he'd better not wake her.

WEDNESDAY, NOVEMBER 3

OFFICE OF THE MEDICAL EXAMINER, ALBANY STREET 8:00 A.M.

The building that housed Dr. Megan Quinn and her staff was an unremarkable, red brick structure with a small sign posted on the exterior wall. The sign itself was rather imposing, if not in size, definitely in description.

Commonwealth of Massachusetts
Office of the Chief Medical Examiner

Danny had only been there twice, during his training days at the academy, but still remembered the smell. A confusing mix of death and disinfectants.

The body of Cary Brennan was laid out on a stainless steel table, covered by a white cloth, except for her feet. Megan Quinn checked the tag, then turned on the overhead microphone before uncovering the body.

65

Being in the morgue hadn't done anything to reduce the obvious brutality of Miss Brennan's death, and now that the blood had been cleaned from around her face, the injuries were even more unsettling. Whatever instrument she had been attacked with, it carried a vicious destructive power.

Megan began. "Autopsy three-eleven-one, cadaver number two-seven-nine. Cary Brennan. Tag confirmed."

Danny stood next to Murphy, both fascinated and slightly repulsed, as the coroner went from head to toe on the body, moving skin flaps, checking for bruising, and using a magnifying glass to search for trace evidence. It was slow, painstaking work and the whole time she was recording her observations.

Murphy had his notepad out and would occasionally write down something the doctor said. For two and a half hours, they watched the coroner work. Much of what he saw, Danny had already forgotten from his visits during his academy days, and it turned out to be a good refresher course.

When she was done, Megan turned the body over to a morgue tech for clean-up, and turned to the detectives. "You guys want to meet me in my office?"

Murph nodded and Danny followed him out of the room. At the other end of a long hallway, they turned into a cramped office, overloaded with books and papers. They each grabbed a chair, and within a few minutes, Megan arrived in street clothes.

She smiled at Danny. "Enjoy the show?"

Danny was proud he hadn't turned green during the process. "Yeah, actually. I learned a lot."

"Good." She sat down behind her desk. "Okay, the preliminary report will be sent to you tomorrow, but here's the gist of it. Cause of death was suffocation by crushing of the trachea. The head trauma likely would have killed her anyway, and whatever was used to beat her up, was probably the same thing used to crush her windpipe. She was restrained at the wrists but I can't ID what was used just yet."

Murphy was furiously scribbling into his notepad. "TOD?"

"I'd put it between two and six in the morning, Monday."

"Well, that fits what we know so far. I saw you did a rape kit. What's your hunch?"

"I didn't see any signs of sexual assault, nor recent intercourse, for that matter. But it will be a while before all the lab samples come back."

"What about the weapon, any guesses?"

Megan shook her head. "Not really. It wasn't large, and it had a smooth surface, but that's about all I can tell you. Sorry."

Murphy stood. "Thanks, Doc. Always entertaining."

Megan laughed. "We do our best to put on a good show."

PRECINCT C-6
1:00 P.M.

Despite having just witnessed an autopsy, Murphy was hungry. They stopped at Mul's for some lunch and Danny surprised himself by being able to eat. When they finally got back to the station, they both hopped on the phone to verify alibis.

Murphy was checking on Joe Turner's whereabouts by requesting his phone records. Danny was doing his best to locate Cary Brennan's ex. He wasn't having any luck. Frustrated, he looked over his notes and realized he hadn't run their victim's prowler reports.

Going into his computer, he searched the previous month for all 10-13 reports in the South Boston area. Though he wasn't sure what he expected, there were seven in the area, and that seemed high. He'd only

handled two or three in all his time on
patrol.

Of the seven, the two involving Cary
Brennan were easy to find. He pulled them
up and printed them off. After retrieving
them, he scanned the reports while walking
back to his desk.

At the bottom of each report was the
responding officer's name. The first report
was filed by Jack Duffy, the officer who'd
found Cary Brennan's body. Danny made a
mental note to ask Duffy about the incident.
The approving supervisor was Lieutenant
Kelly.

The second report stopped him in his
tracks. This one had been handled by a
detective, and the signature belonged to
Raymond Murphy. Danny looked at the
name a second time, then up at his partner
who was on the phone.

*Why didn't he mention this? Surely he'd
remember, wouldn't he?*

Danny didn't know what to do.
Confronting Murphy didn't seem like a good
idea, but letting it drop wasn't a logical step,
either. He folded the reports, returned to his
desk, and put them in the drawer.

Leaning back in his chair, he thought
back over the prowler reports he'd
responded to. Each instance and location of
the 10-13 came back to his memory. Danny

wasn't sure of the details, but he was positive he knew *where* they took place.

What could possibly be the reason for Murph not mentioning the report?

Maybe he was being paranoid, but he held off just the same, deciding to wait for the right time to bring it up. He stood up, tapped Murphy on the shoulder, and pointed toward the door. "Gonna get some air."

Murphy nodded and went back to his call.

Outside, Danny walked along Broadway, enjoying the sun, which had returned minus the wind. It was one of those November days you cherished, and he was in no hurry to go back to the office. He turned down the block toward Mul's Diner and ran into Kevin.

"Hey big shot! How's the detective gig?"

Danny felt a little guilty for not being in touch with his friend. "Good."

"Have a case yet?"

"Yeah, we've been following up on that missing person call you had."

"The Brennan lady?"

"That's the one."

"I heard she was found dead."

Danny nodded. "The next night."

"You got any suspects?"

John C. Dalglish

Danny edged past his friend, ready to continue walking and thinking about the case. "Not at the moment."

"What kind of evidence have you got?"

Danny stopped. "Right now, a bunch of random leads."

"Really? Anything concrete?"

"No, nothing solid."

"What about forensics? Anything from them?"

Danny shook his head, slightly mystified by his friends sudden interest. "Not yet."

"Well, let me know if anything cool comes up, I'd like to follow the case."

"Yeah... okay. See ya later."

"Bye, Buddy. Take care, and say hi to Cass. By the way, when's that baby gonna make his appearance?"

Danny smiled. "Sooner the better in Cassie's book!"

"No doubt!"

When Danny got back to the station, Murphy was away from his desk but a folder was lying open. Danny slid several photographs of the shoe impression from the

71

crime scene aside, and found a one-sheet typed report on what forensics had found.

The impression was made by a size nine-and-a-half shoe. The lab identified it as a boat shoe, specifically a Sperry Top-Sider. There were definite wear patterns and if a pair of shoes matching the description came available, they would be able to run comparisons.

Shoes could be like fingerprints. They had grooves, nicks, and wear spots that could rule out every other shoe but one. It could be very valuable in identifying a suspect, but then Danny would have to prove the suspect was the one wearing them at the crime scene when he committed the crime.

Still, it was something, and Danny did a Google search for Sperry Top-Siders. First made in 1935, they were a well-known and widely used shoe. On the bright side, whoever was wearing them was probably serious about his boating. They weren't cheap.

Murphy returned. "You take a look at the pics?"

"Yeah. Interesting choice of footwear."

Murphy dropped into his chair. "Unfortunately, like Nike basketball shoes don't prove your suspect plays basketball, these don't prove we're looking for a sailor. However, the lab is contacting SoleMate."

"SoleMate?"

"Yeah, it's a database of shoe information. They can usually give you model, manufacture date, sole pattern name. That kind of stuff."

"Nice, but we still need a shoe to compare."

"And there, Danny-boy, is the problem."

"Murphy, Sullivan! Got a minute?"

They both rotated to see the lieutenant leaning out of his office. They filed in and Danny sat but Murphy decided to stand in the doorway. "What's up, Marcus?"

"What have we got so far on the Brennan case?"

Danny was going to pull his notepad out, but Murphy summarized things easily. "Autopsy indicates suffocation by strangulation—her windpipe was crushed—and TOD was early morning Monday. We should have the forensic report first thing tomorrow, but the only leads we have so far are the footprint left at the scene, and a gray sedan seen in the area around the time she disappeared."

"Anything significant on the shoe print?"

"It's a boat shoe, so if we find a suspect with a boating background, it could help."

"Did you check the height characteristics from the shoe?"

Murphy shook his head. "Not yet; only just got the photos."

The lieutenant rotated in his chair and stared at Danny. "How's it going?"

Danny shrugged. "I guess you should ask my trainer."

Kelly laughed. "Don't worry, I already have. Okay you two, we have a briefing with Captain Walsh tomorrow, ten sharp, his office. I'll meet you there."

Both detectives nodded. Kelly's phone rang. "Dismissed."

Danny was still puzzled about something. "Hey Murph, what did he mean by characteristics from the shoe print?"

"The shoe impression can give us an extremely rough estimate of our suspect's height."

"No kidding?"

Murphy laughed. "I wouldn't kid you, Danny-boy!"

Danny rolled his eyes, as Murphy reached into his desk and pulled out a tattered piece of cardboard. "Look, our suspect wears a nine-and-a-half, right?"

Danny nodded.

"So according to the chart, the suspect is between five-eight and six foot, which puts them in a group of about fifteen percent of the population."

"Not much to go on."

Murphy laughed. "Nope, but it's likely we're not looking for a midget or a giant!"

****

Danny looked down at his phone. He'd missed a message from Cass and it was past five o'clock. Both were not good. The file with the crime scene photos had shown up just after Murphy had left, and Danny had been engrossed with them since.

He picked up his phone and called home.

"Hello?"

"Hi Cass, it's me."

"Are you on your way?"

"No, not yet. The crime scene photos came in and I'm going over them."

"When will you be home?"

"Soon. Give me an hour."

Her disappointment was obvious. "Fine. I'll keep dinner warm."

"Thanks, love you."

She'd already hung up.

Somewhat reluctantly, he returned to the photos. So far, he hadn't seen anything that would help them, even in the shots taken after the sun had come up. Nevertheless, he wasn't done and it couldn't wait. At least, he didn't think so.

It was an hour and a half before he finally left for home.

THURSDAY, NOVEMBER 4

PRECINCT C-6
8:45 A.M.

Murphy had called to say he was running behind, and a couple minutes later, the Brennan forensic report had showed up. Danny had been going over the file for the last thirty minutes. There was plenty to review but little to see.

No unidentified hairs were found on the body. No DNA was found under her fingernails, nor anywhere else on her. They'd checked the body for prints, but with the low humidity of fall and the time the body spent outdoors, it had been unlikely they'd find any, and they hadn't. Whoever had done this was good at covering their tracks.

What left Danny most frustrated was the information about the weapon. The description was incredibly vague.

Roughly six inches long, three to five inches wide, hard but with a semi-pliable covering. Victim received a minimum of twenty-five blows to the head, but none were found on the body.

To Danny, the possibilities were mind-boggling. Hundreds of items could be put in a bag or sock or whatever, all of which could leave markings similar those described in the report.

On the other hand, there was no *one* thing that came to mind. At least not something that, by itself, met the parameters. They still had very little to go on.

There was one piece of good news, if he could call it that, and it came in the form of a note attached to an extra photo. Clipped to the back of the folder, in Megan Quinn's handwriting, was the explanation for the close-up photo.

Murphy,
I believe I have identified the restraints I mentioned on scene and in my preliminary. They appear to be double-loop plastic cuffs, wide and likely high-grade. The bruising goes all the way around both wrists, and is wider than your standard zip-tie.

M.Q.

"Hey."

Danny spun in his chair to find his partner sitting down. "Hey yourself. Forensics dropped off the Brennan file."

"Yeah? Anything good?"

Danny shook his head. "Not to my way of thinking. Except we do know what those marks on her wrist probably were."

Danny handed the file to Murphy, who leaned back in his chair. "It's something, but not much. I was hoping not to go to the captain with a bucket full of horse crap."

Murphy's reaction didn't help the case of nerves already building in Danny's gut over the meeting with Captain Walsh. "Did you have any luck with the boyfriends alibi?"

"Well, let's see." Murphy got up and went to the printer, returning moments later with multiple sheets of paper. "These are Turner's phone records."

Danny rolled his chair over to Murphy's desk, and they started working through the day surrounding Cary Brennan's disappearance. Within minutes, they'd found the call from Cary to Joe at eleven-thirty-eight. There wasn't any other activity until six in the morning. That was a missed call from a different number.

Murphy let his finger run across the columns until he got to the cell tower pinged by the missed call. He highlighted it in yellow, then compared it to the call from Cary to Joe earlier that night. "The tower is the same."

Danny nodded. "Yeah, but the TOD was right inside that window, between midnight and early morning, which means he could have been out and back by then."

"True, but it does verify what he's told us so far."

Danny checked the number and dialed. It rang multiple times before going to voice mail. "This is Mike. Leave a message."

"Yes, sir. My name is Detective Sullivan with the Boston Police Department. Please call me when you get this." Danny left his number and hung up. He checked the time. "We need to go."

Murphy looked at his computer, then stood. "Oh joy."

OFFICE OF
CAPTAIN RYAN WALSH
10:03 A.M.

Danny took the chair offered him in the third floor office of Captain Ryan Walsh. Murphy sat next to him. Lieutenant Kelly was already seated by the window and appeared to be relaxed. Danny hoped it was a sign of things to come.

Walsh shut the door and came over to Danny. "Before we start, congratulations are in order." He extended his hand and Danny started to get up. "No need to stand."

They shook hands before the captain turned and went around his desk to sit down. Danny had seen Walsh many times, but never had the opportunity to meet him in person.

The captain's office wasn't small, but the captain managed to shrink the space with his broad shoulders and thick arms. Penetrating brown eyes were partially covered by a pair of glasses that rode the end of his nose, making him look more like a professor than a District Captain.

Walsh opened a file on his desk as he began to talk. "Marcus was just telling me about the case you two are working." Walsh looked up, first at Danny, then at Murphy. "Where are we on it?"

Murphy cleared his throat. "Forensics got their report to us this morning. Unfortunately, there wasn't much to it. They drew a blank on hair, fingerprints, and DNA. The cause of death was confirmed but only a vague description of the weapon was available."

Walsh lifted a page, then another, as if looking for something. Danny was pretty sure he knew everything already, but was getting a feel for his detectives. "No rape, is that right?"

"Yes, sir."

"So the sex offender database won't be much help?"

"It doesn't appear so, but we'll run it anyway."

"What about other suspects?"

Murphy continued. "Only two possibles have surfaced: the boyfriend and an ex-husband."

"Alibis?"

"We've been able to verify a weak one on the boyfriend through phone records, but it doesn't rule him out completely."

The captain looked at Danny. "What about the ex?"

Danny was hoping his voice didn't convey his nerves. "The last known whereabouts was in San Francisco, but I haven't had any luck finding him yet."

Walsh stared at him for a second, then looked at the file. "There was mention of a gray sedan, I believe." Walsh looked at Danny again. "Anything on that?"

Danny shook his head. "Nothing to corroborate it."

"Hmmmm." The captain closed the folder and leaned back in his chair. "Well, Murph, what's your next step?"

"We can do a database search for gray sedans, but I thought we might look at the records from the hospital she worked at first. Maybe we can find somebody that knew her, who also drives a gray sedan."

"Good." The captain hesitated slightly. "Okay, there's something else I need to go over." Danny's heart started to beat a little faster. Like most cops, he didn't like surprises.

Walsh looked at the lieutenant, who had been silent so far, then back at the detectives. "The location of the body poses a problem."

Danny was watching Murphy, whose confusion was obvious on his face. "The Calf Pasture?"

Walsh nodded. "Not so much the Pasture, but what it's next to. The Kennedy Library is getting ready to have a large display tied to the assassination of JFK, running from November 16th through Thanksgiving, and they've asked we not have the crime tape up at after the tenth," The captain paused, but both detectives remained silent. "Anyway, I'm hoping you two can get all your work done before then. Is that a possibility?"

83

Murphy let out a low whistle. "Man, I don't know, Captain. We like to have a scene kept clean for as long as possible, just in case something leads us to search again."

"I know, but do your best. Take more photos, go over the scene several extra times, then let Marcus know when you're finished. Can you do that?"

Murphy shrugged. "Okay." Danny didn't bother agreeing; he knew the decision wasn't one he had any input on.

Walsh rocked forward in his chair. "Excellent. I'll let you two get back to work while Marcus and I chat a little longer."

Danny stood when Murphy did, and they headed for the door. Walsh followed them. "Good to meet you, Sullivan."

"Nice to meet you, sir."

The door closed and Murphy muttered to himself as he headed for the elevator. Danny was trying to catch up. "What's that, Murph?"

"He didn't ask about the shoe print."

"Yeah, that's right. Why not?"

"Because he knew everything he needed before we ever stepped foot in his office."

Danny's suspicion was confirmed. "Then why have us come up?"

"I wish I knew, Sullivan. There never seems to be anything accomplished when I spend time in that man's office."

****

After shutting the door, Walsh leaned against the doorframe and studied his lieutenant. "How's things with Maria?"

Kelly shrugged. "The same."

"You still not living at home?"

Kelly shook his head and stared out the window.

Walsh's heart went out to his friend. "I'm sorry, Marcus."

The lieutenant didn't respond.

Walsh went back to his desk chair. "You know I don't like to interfere with your case assignments, Marcus."

Kelly didn't say anything, waiting for the other shoe to drop.

"You also know I prefer the new detectives get lower grade cases in the beginning of their careers."

"You've mentioned it before."

"The thing is... if the Brennan case doesn't get pushed forward fast enough, I'm gonna hear it from the chief."

Kelly stood and moved toward the door. "You want me to pull the kid off, is that it?"

Walsh rocked back in his chair. "I'm just saying it might be one of those times to make a move."

"Ryan, you know I don't give a rip what City Hall thinks..."

"I know, I know."

"And the case was originally a missing persons, but went south."

"I know that, too."

"I want to leave him on it."

Walsh was quiet for several minutes, staring at Kelly and weighing his options. Finally, he rocked forward. "I'm good with whatever you want, Ryan." He laughed. "Now, get out of my office."

Kelly left, but wasn't laughing.

FRIDAY, NOVEMBER 5

O'BRIEN FUNERAL HOME
DORCHESTER STREET
9:15 A.M.

The funeral for Cary Brennan was set for ten that morning, but the detectives were early. They wanted to find a place to observe the proceedings without being disrespectful of the family. In this case, there was very little family expected.

The funeral home itself was a two-story colonial with a small one-story home attached on the southwest side. Painted a dull brown, it had two dark-brown canvas covers bearing the insignia of the O'Brien Home, one over each set of stairs.

Murphy stopped the car across the street and rolled down the windows. Early November could be quite cold, with lows near freezing and highs barely into the fifties, but the sun was out this morning and it was pleasant. Murphy sipped his coffee as Danny sat next to him with his notepad out.

"Murph?"

"Yeah?"

"I've been meaning to ask you about something."

"So ask."

"Your name is listed as the investigating detective on a prowler report..."

Murphy looked at Danny over the top of his coffee cup. "So?"

Danny fidgeted in his seat. "It was Cary Brennan's house."

Murphy stared at him for a long time. Then to Danny's surprise, he smiled. "I was wondering if you were gonna notice that."

"You were?"

"Yeah. I'd remembered the case as we left the house that first day. I decided I'd wait and see if you followed up on the report."

"Why?"

"A detective has got have the guts to follow a case to wherever or whomever it leads, even if it's his partner."

It was Danny's turn to stare.

Is he for real? He was testing me? It's possible, but then again, he might just be covering his butt.

Murphy had turned back to watching the entrance. "There's the boyfriend."

Danny spotted Joe Turner coming down the side street where he'd parked. "Yeah, he's as close as she has to family, apparently."

Another vehicle parked in front of the funeral home and Carol Nelson got out. Two other women riding with her also climbed out. All three wore their nurse uniforms. Murphy pointed at the three. "We need to ask the supervisor who those other two women are, just for the record."

The next car to arrive piqued both detectives' interest. A plain, light-colored sedan bearing a Hertz rental sticker and driven by a man. After parking, he climbed out and locked the door. He was thin and easily over six feet tall, with black hair tinged and a dark tan, Danny immediately suspected who it might be.

"Think that's Alex Brennan?"

Murphy opened his door. "I don't know, but let's follow him in and see what name he puts on the registry."

Dodging a bit of traffic, the two detectives crossed the road and followed the man up the stairs. Murphy didn't make contact, and Danny hung back as well. The inside of the home was considerably darker than the bright sunshine outside, and it took several seconds for their eyes to adjust.

A man wearing a suit with the O'Brien insignia on the lapel was directing people to sign the registry book, and then pointing them toward the main room. They waited their turn behind the man from outside, then stepped forward together. They both read the name, then looked at each other. "That's him." Murphy started to follow him into the sanctuary.

Danny hesitated. "Should I sign?"

Murphy was gone, so Danny decided it was the right thing to do. He signed both their names with the designation "BPD" next to the signatures. Following Murphy, he came into a dimly lit room, several times longer than it was wide, with rows of chairs on both sides of a center aisle. Danny didn't see his partner immediately, but eventually spotted him against the wall, halfway toward the front.

A vaguely familiar hymn came from the overhead sound system as he made his way to where Murphy sat. Sliding in next to his partner, he took a closer look at the room. Alex Brennan was at the front, standing over his ex-wife's casket, head bowed. The coffin was closed, undoubtedly because of the injuries, and had a large spray of roses on top.

More people filed in, and Danny did his best to make note of everyone there. Most appeared to be in the medical field and were probably acquaintances from the hospital.

Danny checked to make sure his phones were off and noted the time. Ten exactly.

A man wearing a black robe with a purple silk scarf that hung to his knees, walked up to the lectern. He opened his Bible and the music stopped. A hush fell across the room for the next half hour, broken only by the speaking of the pastor, and a couple hymns.

Amazing Grace was played last and the service ended. Danny stood and turned to look toward the door, checking to make sure he hadn't missed anyone. To his surprise, Jack Duffy, dressed in street clothes, was just leaving. Danny hurried to catch up with him.

Outside, Jack was getting into a silver Toyota. "Jack!"

Duffy looked up and waved. "Hey, Danny."

"Hold up!"

Duffy climbed into his car, then rolled down the window. When Danny walked up, the officer looked uncomfortable. "Nice service, huh?"

Danny nodded. "I'm a little surprised to see you here."

The officer didn't meet Danny's gaze. "Aww, you know. I found her, so I thought I'd pay my respects, that's all."

Danny suspected he was hiding something, but couldn't imagine what it might be. "Oh, well, that's nice of you."

"I go on duty in an hour, so I better run."

"Sure. See ya, Jack."

Danny watched him drive away, bothered by the conversation, but unsure why. It was then he remembered Alex Brennan. Turning and going back inside, he found Murphy and Brennan talking in a side hallway.

"Mr. Brennan, this is my partner, Detective Sullivan."

The man nodded toward Danny, and it was obvious he'd been crying. Danny was surprised, considering the time Alex and Cary Brennan had supposedly been apart. "I'm sorry for your loss, Mr. Brennan."

"Alex, please."

Murphy had his notepad out. "When will you be leaving town, sir?"

"I'll be catching a flight tomorrow morning."

"And where were you last Sunday night?"

"My home in San Diego."

"Do you have anyone that can lock that down for us?"

Alex nodded. "You can call my boss. I worked last Sunday. I'm a waiter at

Bandar's Restaurant." He recited the number from memory.

Danny couldn't help himself. "I thought you were in San Francisco?"

"At one time."

"When did you move to San Diego?"

"Last year."

Danny nodded. "You seem broken up, forgive me for saying so, but rarely are divorced couples so close."

Murphy stopped writing and stared at Danny, who ignored the glare. Alex seemed unbothered by the question. "You have to understand, Detective. Cary went through a difficult time with me, and when I discovered I'd made a mistake, I reached out to her. She was a remarkable lady, and we just stayed in touch."

"Joe Turner said you hadn't talked to her in years."

"She didn't want him to know. She felt it was simpler that way."

Danny was touched by the story, glad to see some people can get past the hurt, if it was true. He shook Alex's hand. "Again, I'm sorry for your loss."

"Thank you."

Apparently satisfied, Murphy put away his pad. "Thank you for your time, Mr. Brennan."

They walked back out into the sunshine, then to their car. Murphy opened the door, then looked across the roof at Danny. "Now, the fun begins!"

"The fun?"

"Paperwork."

"Oh, that fun."

PRECINCT C-6
1:00 P.M.

Murphy had gone to Boston Medical to get vehicle information, hoping to find the names of any employees with a gray sedan. He was probably going to be gone all afternoon. Danny had sat at his desk since lunch doing a search of sex offenders in the South Boston area. There were only twenty-one registered as such, a surprise to him, but he pulled each file.

The sex offenders needed to be cleared, but because the victim wasn't raped, both detectives agreed the crime didn't fit the description of a typical offender. Nevertheless, Danny started by plotting their addresses on a city map. Next, he checked each name for recent arrests. Eleven names were immediately eliminated because they were back in prison. Six for parole violations and five for new crimes.

The type of crime ruled out seven of the remaining ten. They were child pornography convictions, with no record of attacks on adult women. That left him three. He checked the addresses, looked at his watch, and decided there was no time like the present. He picked the closest address and headed out.

****

Danny arrived back at the precinct just before six-thirty. He'd managed to find and question all three men on his list. It had been exhausting and frustrating.

The first man claimed to be at work, which was verified by his boss. The second was at a family get-together until well past midnight on Sunday, verified by at least three family members. The third was at a church overnight lock-in. The pastor confirmed it.

Murphy was at his desk when Danny came in. "Any luck?"

"None. As we suspected, the sex offender list was a dead end."

Murphy nodded. "Don't feel bad. The hospital gave me the names of six people with gray sedans registered in their parking permit files. Five were women, two of which were married, but claimed their husbands hadn't driven their cars in months. The other three women said they hadn't loaned their car to anyone."

"What about the sixth name?"

"Harry Logan, five foot-six and sixty-four years old. Part-time janitor."

Danny dropped into his chair. "Couldn't have had the strength to carry out the crime, at least not alone. And the shoe print doesn't fit."

"That was my feeling, but I talked to him anyway. He was working the overnight at the hospital that Sunday, and there are at least four shots of him on security cameras between midnight and six in the morning."

"Dang, Murph. We're not getting anywhere!"

Murph nodded. "Sometimes it's like that... until it's not."

Danny laughed. "What's your plan for tomorrow?"

"I've got something to take care of out of town. I won't be back until Monday."

"Well, there isn't much else to do, not until we get another lead. I guess I'll see you Monday morning."

SULLIVAN RESIDENCE
WEST ROXBURY
7:25 P.M.

Danny came through the door to the sound of the microwave heating his dinner. He was ravenous, and though he couldn't identify it, the aroma made his stomach rumble. "Cass?"

"In here."

He followed the hallway back to their bedroom, finding Cass lying on her side in bed. "Are you okay?"

She gave him a weary smile. "Yeah. Junior's been kicking all day and my back is sore. I just wanted to lie down for a few minutes."

Danny took off his work clothes and slipped into a sweatshirt and jogging pants. Dropping gingerly onto the bed next to Cass, he kissed her, then laid his hand on her stomach. Within seconds, he felt a thump. Followed by several more. "Wow! You weren't kidding. You think he wants to come out?"

"I think *she* will be out when *she* is ready, but not yet."

"Just like a woman; can't decide!"

97

She reached over and punched his shoulder, sending him rolling onto his back. "You're lucky I'm pregnant or I would make you regret those words."

He laughed, then closed his eyes. He fell asleep without ever discovering what was for dinner.

SATURDAY, NOVEMBER 6

GATES OF HEAVEN
CATHOLIC CHURCH
4:50 P.M.

Danny stood outside the huge edifice that was Gates of Heaven, a towering brick building with the trademark stained glass and multiple towers, giving it a distinctly castle-like feel. The church and accompanying school next door took up an entire city block.

He was waiting on Cassie, who had stopped to talk to the priest about the impending birth. Danny had decided to wait in the sunshine outside. He and Cass had gone over to his parents' for a Saturday brunch, then watched the Notre Dame football game on TV.

At halftime, he'd gotten up to get something to drink, and his mother had cornered him in the kitchen.

"Danny, are you and Cassie going to mass today?"

"I don't know, Mom. I guess it depends on how she's feeling?"

"I just checked with her and she thinks it's a good idea."

"Okay then, I guess we're going to mass. Is Pop going?"

She laughed. "Oh, yeah. He's going, whether he likes it or not. We don't get to attend as a familyt often."

It wasn't that Danny didn't want to go, he'd been brought up in the church, but time with Cassie was precious these days. Soon, they would be parents of a newborn and all that entailed, which meant less time for just them. When he threw in how much time the Brennan case was taking, he hardly got to see her as it was.

He watched as she came down the front steps of the church, clutching the railing tightly, and trying to see over her bulging stomach to where her feet were going. He hadn't been able to decide if she was more beautiful now or before she got pregnant, not that he thought about it much, but she had posed the question to him during her seventh month.

"I look like a cow!

She was standing in front of a mirror in the maternity section of J.C. Penney. He was sitting on one of those rolling stools used to reach a top shelf, watching her go in and out of the changing room.

"You do not! You're beautiful."

"You have to say that."

"Oh, do I now?"

"Of course. Otherwise, you know I'll hurt you in your sleep!"

He laughed. "Although that may be true, I stick by my statement."

On their way home in the car, a serious expression took control of her face, and she posed the question.

"Do you wish I was back to my skinny self?"

Danny was about to crack a joke along the lines of "now that you mention it," but she was feeling insecure, and decided it in bad taste. He slid his hand across the front seat and laced his fingers through hers.

"Cassie Sullivan, you are as beautiful right now as any time I've ever looked at you."

She'd teared up slightly, then brought his hand to her lips. "Thank you, but it scares me how good a liar you are!"

He met her at the bottom step and helped her toward the car. He'd already said goodbye to his mother and father, and wanted nothing more than a quiet night with Cass. Now, if he could just stay awake.

BOSTON HOMICIDE

SUNDAY, NOVEMBER 7

SHENANNIGANS
BAR AND GRILL
12:45 A.M.

Described as a contemporary bar and eatery with Irish flair, Shenannigans' took up the bottom floor of a four-story brownstone apartment building, and stayed open each night until one in the morning. Lisa Nolan stopped her friend.

"I don't have any tables left and I've finished my side work, is it okay if I take off?"

"Yeah, I'll take it from here."

"Are you sure you don't mind, Cindy?"

"No, no... It's fine. I've got a party that will be here until past closing anyway."

"Thanks so much. I'm beat."

"You're welcome so much. See ya tomorrow."

Lisa Nolan undid her apron and headed for the back of the restaurant. Like most Saturday nights into Sunday mornings at the pub, it had been chaotic. Even though she made her best money on nights like that, she wasn't as young as she used to be.

At forty-one, she still had her figure, despite the fact she wasn't one to work out at a gym, and the younger men in the bar still flirted with her. She'd been blessed with her mother's blonde hair and brown eyes, as well as her father's wide smile. Still, after nearly nine hours on her feet, she was exhausted.

Home was just eight blocks from the restaurant, so she zipped her Celtics jacket all the way up and stepped out into the early morning. The wind whipped at her hair and reddened her face. There were still bar patrons out, and an occasional car would go by on E Street, but she was alone as she approached Tudor Street and her home.

Taking out her keys, she opened the door and stepped inside.

"Hey there!"

Lisa turned to see a car stopped by the curb.

"Lisa!"

She didn't recognize the car, but the driver got out and appeared vaguely familiar. "I'm sorry, I don't remember you."

The man wore a broad smile and came right up to her. "Remember me now?"

"Oh... sure, you're..."

A bright flash raced across her vision and pain coursed through her body. She collapsed, fear competing with the pain, until she blacked out.

SHENANNIGANS
BAR AND GRILL
2:30 P.M.

All ten of the restaurant's TVs were tuned to NFL football, over half of them showing the hometown Patriots game. Cindy put her purse in her locker and donned her apron. At the bar, she found the manager, Tony Burns. "Hey, TB."

"Hey, Cindy."

"What's the score?"

"Patriots by seven. Have you heard from Lisa?"

Cindy looked around the restaurant, as if Lisa would be right there, and Tony was blind. "She's not here yet?"

"Nope."

"And she didn't call?"

"Again, nope."

Cindy's face immediately reflected the concern she felt. "She was due in at one, right?"

"Yeah, but no show."

Lisa reached into her back pocket and took out her phone. "Let me try her."

After several rings, her friend's voice came on. "This is Lisa. I'm either busy or ignoring you. Leave a message if you want, bye."

"Lisa, this is Cindy. Where are you? Call me as soon as you get this, okay?"

She hung up and shrugged at Tony. "I can't imagine where she'd be. She never misses a shift."

"I know. That's what I was thinking."

LISA NOLAN'S APARTMENT
TUDOR STREET
5:40 P.M.

Cindy banged on the door for a second time. "Lisa!"

There was no sound from inside and the door was locked. She had taken a half-hour break, with encouragement from Tony, to run over to her friend's studio apartment.

Moving around to the small window on the backside of the apartment, and using her hand to shield against the glare, Cindy peered through the window. There was no sign of her friend, nor anything out of place.

She banged on the glass. "Lisa?"

The house was silent.

Checking her watch, she realized she needed to head back. Dialing Lisa's number for the fourth time in the last three hours, she left another message.

"Lisa, I'm getting worried. I'm outside your apartment and I can't find you. Call me, please."

She hurried back along E Street, hoping Lisa may have shown up at the restaurant while she was gone looking for her.

BOSTON HOMICIDE

MONDAY, NOVEMBER 8

LISA NOLAN'S APARTMENT
7:30 A.M.

Cindy had gone home after work and tried to sleep, but to no avail. She got up and came back to her friend's apartment, this time pounding louder and yelling. The disturbance didn't bring Lisa to the door, but it did wake up the landlord, who lived in the house attached to the studio apartment.

"What's going on?"

Cindy had met the landlord several times. "Oh, Mr. O'Connell, have you seen Lisa?"

"I saw her on Saturday morning. Why?"

Cindy was at the point of tears. "I saw her at work on Saturday night, but no one has seen or heard from her since."

"Well, she's a grown woman. Maybe she had something to take care of."

"No... Something is wrong! She missed work yesterday without calling, and she never does that."

The elderly man frowned. "Settle down now, Cindy. I'm sure there's a reasonable explanation. Let me go get my key."

A few minutes later, the landlord returned. It took him a minute to maneuver unlocking the door, but when he did, he couldn't get it open. Something was behind it. Cindy came forward and leaned against the door. It slid open.

The items blocking the door were a purse and a single shoe, which had become jammed under the bottom.

Cindy's heart was already pounding, and when she saw the purse, panic began to rise from deep inside her. "Lisa? Lisa!"

Mr. O'Connell had followed her in. "Miss Nolan?"

It was a studio, and the only room with a door was the bathroom. Cindy crossed to it and slowly pushed it open. It creaked loudly as it moved backward until it bumped against the bathtub. Cindy, with her eyes half-closed from fear, looked into the tub.

She took a deep breath. "She's not in here!"

"Would she go anywhere without her purse?"

Cindy walked over and took the purse from Mr. O'Connell. "Definitely not."

When she opened it, Lisa's cellphone was inside. Cindy tried to turn it on but it was dead. Looking down at the shoe stuck under the door, a chill ran through her.

"That's one of the shoes she was wearing at work Saturday night."

The landlord scanned the room, looking for the other shoe. "I don't see the matching one, do you?"

Cindy shook her head, tears welling up in her eyes. "What do we do?"

Mr. O'Connell was already on his way out the door. "Call the police, that's what."

PRECINCT C-6
7:55 A.M.

Danny arrived Monday morning to find Murphy's desk still empty. He grabbed the file and started looking at the phone records for Joe Turner. They needed to rule him either in or out as a suspect.

They knew he'd talked to Cary Brennan around midnight, and that he'd missed a call around six in the morning. There had to be something more. Danny flipped to the next page, but it was blank.

Where's the text message history?

He got up and rummaged through some of the mess on Murphy's desk, but couldn't find it.

"Lose something?"

Danny looked up with a start. "Oh...No...Well, kinda."

Murphy gave him a funny look. "So, this thing you kinda lost, was it lost on my desk?"

Danny laughed nervously. "No, I mean I don't know. I was looking for the text message records from Joe Turner's phone."

Murphy looked at the file on Danny's desk. "It's in there, isn't it?"

"No. Just the phone records and a blank sheet."

"Well, maybe he didn't have any text messages?"

Danny moved back over to his own desk. "Maybe..."

Murphy sat down. "Just to be sure, I'll call and make sure someone didn't drop the ball."

"Sounds good. How was your weekend?"

Murphy shrugged. "Uneventful. You?"

"Good. Managed to catch up on a little sleep."

"Nice."

"Did you get your out-of-town business taken care of?"

"Yeah... All good."

Murphy picked up the phone and dialed. Danny went to get a cup of coffee, and when he returned a few minutes later, Murphy was off the phone. "They said we didn't request the text message record, just phone calls."

Danny sipped his coffee, then scowled. "Since when do you have to request them separately?"

"That's what I said. Anyway, they're supposed to send them over shortly."

"Good."

LISA NOLAN'S APARTMENT
8:10 A.M.

It took nearly a half-hour for an officer to respond to the 9-1-1 call placed by Mr. O'Connell. In the meantime, Lisa and the landlord had stayed outside, just in case they touched something they shouldn't. They both stood when the blue and white car pulled up.

The officer got out, put on his jacket, and came around to where they stood. "You called in a missing persons report?"

The landlord raised his hand. "I did, Officer."

The patrolman, whose badge identified him as Officer Duffy, took out a notepad and pencil. "And your name?"

"Thomas O'Connell, I own the apartment."

Duffy nodded at Cindy. "And you are?"

"Cindy Reid, it's my friend who's missing."

"And what's her name?"

"Lisa Nolan."

"When was the last time she was seen?"

"Saturday night, well actually, early Sunday morning when she left work."

"Where is work?"

"Shenannigans' on Broadway."

The officer smiled. "Good food there." He stopped writing and scanned the area. "Is this her residence?"

"Yes."

"Car?"

Cindy shook her head. "She walks to and from work. I believe she takes busses everywhere else."

Duffy made one last note, then put away the pad. "Have you been inside?"

"Yes, but only briefly."

"Okay, wait out here. I'm going to look around."

O'Connell and Cindy sat down again as the officer went inside. He came out a few minutes later. "Do you know where her other shoe is?"

Lisa shook her head. "And she never goes anywhere without her purse and cellphone."

"Okay, you two remain outside. I'm going to request back-up."

LIEUTENANT KELLY'S OFFICE
8:35 A.M.

Only halfway through his second cup of coffee, Marcus Kelly could feel a headache coming on. His phone rang for the fourth time in a row.

"Kelly!"

"Lieutenant, this is dispatch. We have a request for a detective."

"What was the original call?"

"Missing persons. The responding officer suspects foul play."

"Where?"

"Tudor and E Street."

Kelly placed it on a mental map. "Okay, give me the address?"

He jotted it down and hung up. Murphy happened by the office door carrying a stack of papers. "Hey, Murph!"

The detective backed up and stuck his head in the door. "Yeah, Lieutenant?"

"What are you working on?"

"We're trying to pin down the boyfriend's alibi from the Brennan case."

The lieutenant stood and went to the door, handing the note to Murphy. "You and Sullivan check this out. It's a missing persons with suspicious circumstances, and it's just around the corner from the Brennan place."

Murphy looked down at the note. "Will do."

LISA NOLAN'S APARTMENT 9:45 A.M.

Murphy parked behind the blue and white patrol car on Tudor. The apartment, which was really a small single-story addition to the back of a row house, had a partial privacy fence and faced an alley. It was immediately apparent this was a good place to snatch someone.

Danny took out his notepad as Jack Duffy approached. "Hey, Danny."

"Hi Jack. We need to stop meeting like this."

Duffy smiled. "Indeed."

Murphy joined them. "What have we got?"

"Lisa Nolan, forty-one, last seen around one Sunday morning. Not answering calls and missed work yesterday."

"Who reported it?"

"The landlord, Mr. O'Connell, and a friend, Cindy Reid."

"Have you been inside?"

Duffy nodded. "Residence was locked. Landlord went in and then called. The missing woman's purse and cellphone are inside, along with one shoe."

Murphy's eyebrows went up. "One?"

"Yes. The items were just inside the door, and the other shoe has not been found."

"Okay, Officer. We'll take it from here. Can I get you to tape off the entrance to the yard?"

"Yes, sir."

Danny looked over at the two people standing by the apartment entrance. "Murph, you want to take the landlord and I'll speak with the friend?"

"That'll work."

Danny went over to the young lady who sat on the front step. "Miss Reid?"

"Yes?"

"I'm Detective Sullivan. May I ask you a few questions?"

"Sure."

Danny pointed toward the far end of the yard. "Let's go over here."

He waited for her to stand, then led her over to where they could speak in private. "Miss Reid..."

"Cindy."

"Cindy, when was the last time you saw Miss Nolan?"

"Probably twelve-forty-five Sunday morning. The bar closes at one and she wanted to head out a little early. I told her I would close up."

"The bar?"

"Shenannigans'. It's over on Broadway."

Danny nodded. "I know it. I've eaten there a few times. When did you first realize your friend was missing?"

"I came in for work yesterday and she hadn't shown. That's not like her. I came by yesterday evening on my break and got no answer."

"Did you try the door?"

"Yes. It was locked."

"Can you think of anyone who would want to hurt Miss Nolan?"

Cindy shook her head. "No one. She is as sweet a person as I've ever met."

"What about a boyfriend or ex?"

Another shake of the head. "She's not dating anyone that I know of and her husband died in a car wreck more than ten years ago."

Danny finished writing and closed his pad. "Do you have a picture of your friend?"

Cindy opened her purse and pulled out a wallet. She produced a photo and handed it to Danny. "That's her and I last month. We were out having a few drinks."

Danny stared at the picture. He'd seen that face, or at least one just like it, recently. Lisa Nolan was almost a dead ringer for Cary Brennan. A chill crawled its way up his spine and apparently Cindy noticed.

"Do you know her?"

Danny forced a smile. "No. She just looks like somebody I know. Can I keep this for now?"

"Sure."

Danny took out his new detective cards and handed one to Cindy. "Let me know if you think of anything or hear from your friend."

"I will."

Danny left her there and caught up with Murphy, who was inside the apartment. "What have you found, Murph?"

"Not a lot. I plugged the missing woman's phone in to charge and I've been looking for the other shoe."

Danny looked around the small studio. "The friend said the door was locked. If her purse was inside, then her keys should be

119

also, unless she took them with her when she left."

"True." Murphy walked to the door and played with the lock. "Not pried on that I can see. It's one of those automatic jobs that snaps shut when the door closes."

Danny had dropped to his knees and was shining his flashlight under the furniture. The sleeper sofa was open and the sheets still a mess, but with no blood or broken debris, it seemed to indicate there wasn't a struggle. He stood back up. "No keys, no shoe."

Murphy went to the bathroom, looking around behind the door, as Danny went to look at the front entrance. The automatic lock wasn't very substantial, but Murphy appeared to be correct—there was no sign of the lock being forced. A flash caught his eye.

Going out onto the top step, he waved his hand over the grass, moving it with the breeze from his palm. The flash came again. The sun was reflecting off a set of keys. "Murph!"

Taking his pencil, Danny ran it through the loop and lifted the keys out of the grass. Murphy appeared at the door. "Find something?"

"Keys."

Murphy eyed the key fob hanging from Danny's pencil. "There's a gold L on them. I'd say they belong to our girl."

"Yeah, but why are they outside?"

Murphy looked back at the floor in the entrance, then at the spot where Danny found the keys. "The purse and shoe were on the floor just inside the door. The keys were just outside. My guess is she was attacked standing in the open doorway."

Danny produced an evidence bag and dropped the keys in. "So, you're thinking foul play?"

"I am."

Danny pulled out the photo Cindy Reid had given him. "Take a look at this."

Murphy stared at the picture, then looked over the top of it at his partner. "Let's get a forensic team out here."

An hour later, the small apartment was crawling with forensic techs. Danny was standing in the little kitchenette area and looking out the window. Sitting on the window ledge, partially concealed by a scouring pad, was a Boston Police

Department card. Danny picked it up and read the name.

> *Lieutenant Marcus Kelly*
> *Major Case Squad*
> *South Boston Precinct C-6*

Danny stared at it for a minute, trying to make sense of the discovery. Not wanting to leave it alone, nor to make a big deal out of it, he finally decided to tuck it into his shirt pocket and ask the lieutenant himself.

Murphy walked up. "Neighborhood canvas has begun, so we'll need to follow up tonight with the 'nobody home' addresses."

Danny thought about mentioning the card to Murphy, but he wasn't sure he could do so without it sounding like he was making innuendos about the lieutenant, which didn't seem to be very smart. "Sounds like a big time! I'll have to let Cassie know."

Murphy gave him a wry smile. "Fortunately, I don't have to do that anymore."

Danny realized he knew very little about his partner's personal life. "Nobody at home, Murph?"

His partner shook his head. "Been divorced for thirteen years. Never found anyone else who could put up with my personality."

Danny laughed. "I bet! I have a hard enough time putting up with you for half the day. I can't imagine you for twenty-four hours."

Murphy smiled. "You're not my type anyway, Sullivan."

SULLIVAN RESIDENCE
WEST ROXBURY
10:10 P.M.

Danny cut his headlights as he pulled into the driveway. Turning the car off, he was too tired to get out. He and Murphy had just spent over three hours knocking on doors around the Nolan apartment, mostly to no avail. The majority of people Danny talked to said they didn't know who lived in the small studio apartment, and some didn't even know there *was* an apartment back there.

Murphy had found one person, a lady who lived alone just down the street, who had seen a prowler one night not long ago. She wasn't sure if it was last week or the week before, and she hadn't bothered to call the police because she wasn't sure he was a prowler.

"He could've just been a strange person who didn't mean any harm."

Murphy was of the opinion the woman was the "strange one who doesn't mean any harm." Danny put more credence to the suggestion someone might have been lurking around, especially with the events of late, but it still didn't do them any good.

An outside porch light came on and the front door opened. Standing behind the storm door, watching him sit there, was Cassie. She had on a floor-length flannel nightgown that protruded distinctly at her mid-section.

He climbed out and went to the door, which she opened for him. Stepping inside, he wrapped his arms around her and savored her warmth. He missed being home with her every night, and the laughs they would share. He missed his best friend.

He whispered in her ear. "I love you."

She looked up and kissed him. "I love you, more."

John C. Dalglish

TUESDAY, NOVEMBER 9

PRECINCT C-6
7:45 A.M.

Danny was just pulling into the parking lot when his phone rang. "Sullivan. Where are you?"

"Morning, Murph."

"Morning. Where are you?"

"Parking lot."

"Good. I'm on my way down."

The line went dead and Danny was left staring at his phone.

What now?

A few minutes later, Murphy came walking outside and climbed into Danny's car. "They found our girl."

"Where?"

"Harborwalk on Columbia Point."

"Is she okay?"

"She's dead. Same method as the Brennan woman."

Danny put the car in drive and headed for the waterfront.

Columbia Point was in the same area where they'd found Cary Brennan, near the John Kennedy Library, but on the opposite

125

side. Danny could almost feel the heat being turned up as they tried to get a handle on these cases.

Perhaps subconsciously, he rubbed the back of his neck.

COLUMBIA POINT
SOUTH BOSTON
8:30 A.M.

Coming across University Drive, they passed in front of the large UMass Campus Center Circle Lawn, which is backed by the semi-circle building familiar to all University of Massachusetts alums. Students came and went on the huge green expanse, unaware of the horror just blocks away. Danny almost envied them.

University Drive changed to Columbia Point Road, which led across the waterfront up to the entrance of the JFK Library. Midway between the college and the library, they came upon the crime tape flapping in the onshore breeze. Lights from the top of several police vehicles repeated their blinking pattern, subdued by the bright sunshine.

Stopping about twenty yards from the tape, they got out of the car and walked up to the police perimeter. Danny was surprised to see Kevin there. "Hey, Buddy. How did you draw 'body-guard' duty?"

"Just lucky, I guess. I was the one who found her."

Danny took out his notepad as Murphy indicated he would go on to the scene. "How'd you find her?"

"I like to come down here in the morning at the start of my shift. Just wander the Harborwalk before going on vehicle patrol."

"I see." Danny didn't see. He couldn't remember his friend ever doing that, but maybe it was a new habit. "Notice anyone around?"

"No, not a soul."

"Okay, thanks."

Danny shook his friend's hand and ducked under the tape.

He found Murphy consulting with Megan Quinn. Danny's worst fear was confirmed as soon as he spotted the body of Lisa Nolan. She was naked, legs and arms spread wide, and her face was a bloody mess. They were almost certainly hunting a serial killer. Only the autopsy was left to confirm it, but Danny didn't need a report to tell him what he could see.

127

The body was in the grass, only yards
from the white concrete pillars that separate
the edge of the Harborwalk from the grass,
and the beach beyond. He could see the
Kennedy Library rising from just beyond the
parking lot on the other side of the
Harborwalk.

Murphy finished his conversation and
came over to where Danny stood. "As you
can probably tell, it's a match to the
Brennan scene."

"Pretty obvious."

"Megan says the wrists have the same
bruising, and at first glance, she's guessing
no sexual assault."

"I guess that likely rules out Joe
Turner?"

"Probably, but we'll still need to find
out where he was this morning."

"This morning?"

"Yeah. Quinn guessed the TOD to be
roughly thirty-six hours ago, but Officer
Doyle said he does a walk every morning
and she wasn't here yesterday."

"Makes sense. She'd be hard to miss for
people jogging and riding bikes all day
yesterday."

"Right, so this is just a dump site."

Danny looked at the ocean, lapping
steadily only feet from the body, and was
struck by the disconnect between the land

and the sea. The beauty of the water against ugliness of the murder.

Do you ever get used to this?

"What's that?"

Danny realized he'd been thinking out loud. "Do you ever get used to this?"

Murphy looked at Danny, then at the body of Lisa Nolan. "I don't know how you could."

PRECINCT C-6
11:00 A.M.

A search of the entire area around where Lisa Nolan was found yielded no new evidence. Not even a shoeprint this time around.

Murphy was on the phone with Joe Turner when Danny noticed the lieutenant was alone in his office. He felt for the card in his pocket, then went over to the office door, knocking lightly on the doorframe. "Lieutenant?"

"Sullivan. What can I do for you?"

"Got a minute?"

"Sure. Come in, shut the door."

Danny did, then pulled the card out of his pocket. "I found this the other day at our latest victim's apartment. "

Kelly took the card and leaned back in his chair, his eyes fixed on the name in front of him. "This is one of mine."

"Yes, sir. It was on a shelf. I felt it wise to ask you myself."

Kelly nodded. "Does Murph know you found this?"

"No, sir."

Kelly was quiet for a moment, still staring at the card. "What's her name?"

"Lisa Nolan."

"Do you have a photo of her?"

"Yes. I'll be right back."

Danny went to his desk and returned with the photo he had secured from Cindy Reid. "This is her."

Kelly stared at it for a minute longer, then began to smile. "Oh, of course. The name didn't ring a bell but I remember her face. She came in at the end of October, late in the evening on a Thursday or Friday. She wanted to report a prowler, but all the detectives were gone."

"Really? What did she say?"

"As I recall, she wasn't sure of the exact day it happened and didn't get a look at him, so she decided against filing it."

"That's too bad."

The lieutenant stood. "It's good work following up on everything, no matter how small."

"Yes, sir."

Kelly opened the door. "Keep me updated if you find anything else, okay?"

Danny stepped out of the office. "Of course."

The door started to close, but Danny leaned back in. "Can I have that, sir? I need to enter it into evidence."

"Oh, of course. Here."

Danny took the card. "Nothing personal, you understand how it is."

"Absolutely."

The door closed and Danny returned to his desk. Murphy was just getting off the phone. "Joe Turner was out of town the past two days. Confirmed it with the hotel he stayed in."

Danny dropped into his chair, still troubled by the exchange with the lieutenant. "So, what now?"

"Lunch."

Danny shrugged. "Not real hungry. You go."

Murphy gave him a sideways glance, then stood up. "Suit yourself. Back in a while."

"Thanks for the warning."

Murphy rolled his eyes and headed out of the squad room.

Danny turned to his computer and ran a search on Lisa Nolan. To his surprise, it popped up a prowler report. The responding officer was Kevin Doyle, but it was just a week ago. On a hunch, Danny ran a search for all 10-13 reports filed in the months of September and October. Eleven incidences were catalogued.

Next, he ran the same search for the months of July and August. Just two showed up.

That doesn't make sense. The warmer months figure to be the worst for that kind activity.

Finally, he ran one more search, this time for the last twelve months. He stared at the number, not sure it was correct. Southie had nineteen prowler calls in the past year, and eleven of them were in the last two months.

Is it coincidence? Maybe.

The voice of his father echoed in his mind. *"I don't like coincidences around dead bodies."*

Danny could see why. They don't feel right.

He printed off the results from all three searches, retrieved them, and laid them out on his desk. Taking a yellow marker, he highlighted the date, the name of the person reporting it, and the responding officer. Another disturbing pattern emerged.

Of the nineteen incidents, seven were handled by Jack Duffy, four by Kevin Doyle, and two by Murphy.

More coincidence?

He checked the other six cases and found them all handled by different officers, none of which he recognized. A very uncomfortable thought started clawing at the back Danny's mind.

OFFICE OF
THE MEDICAL EXAMINER
ALBANY STREET
1:45 P.M.

For the second time in less than a week, Danny and his partner stood quietly watching an autopsy. When it was over, they met the coroner in her office as before. The similarities to the last one they observed were obvious, and Megan Quinn ticked them off as she read from her notes.

"Width of the wrist bruises, and the exact location of them, matches Cary Brennan. Injuries to the face and head match those of Cary Brennan, and were likely made by the same object. There was no evidence of sexual assault and no trace evidence was recovered."

Both detectives were making notes on their pads as she spoke. Her next statement forced both of them to look up.

"There were two big differences, however. First, the cause of death was manual strangulation, not a crushed windpipe. This killing was done by hand, or rather it appears by gloves."

Danny wrote it down but Murphy remained focused on the coroner. "What's the second?"

"I found two bruises on the back of the neck that were consistent with a Taser burn."

"You're joking?"

"I don't joke about this stuff, Murph. Here, see for yourself." She tossed a photo on the desk.

Danny looked it over, and the two spots were clearly different from any of the other markings on the victim. "What about Cary Brennan's body?"

Megan looked at Danny, nodding slowly. "My thought exactly. I'll review the autopsy photos and see if I missed similar marks on her. If I did, they're likely hidden by some of the bruising."

Murphy handed the photo back. "That explains how the victim was subdued."

"Indeed. Oh, and one more thing."

Both detectives stared at her expectantly. "The manner of death was homicide."

Murphy chuckled. "I thought you said you don't joke about such matters."

Quinn's face remained serious. "I don't." A few seconds later, her ability to stop from smiling abandoned her, a she broke into a wide grin. "See ya next time, gentlemen."

Murphy grunted. "If there's a next time!"

"Oh, there will be. In my business, there's always a next time."

LIEUTENANT KELLY'S OFFICE
4:20 P.M.

Marcus Kelly dialed the number on his cellphone for the third time in an hour. He still got no answer, and for the third time, he left a message.

"Please call me when you get this. It's very important."

He hung up just as his office phone rang. "Lieutenant Kelly."

"Marcus, this is Walsh."

135

"Hey, Cap. To what do I owe the pleasure?"

"I understand you have another body on your hands from the JFK Library area, is that right?"

"I'm afraid so. Murphy and Sullivan were at the autopsy this afternoon."

"Are they connected?"

"According to Megan Quinn, they are."

There were several moments of silence, then it sounded to Kelly like his boss had come to a decision. "Let's do this. Call Grace Sheehan over at the BAU, tell her the situation, and see if she thinks she can help us."

Kelly had already considered bringing in an agent from the FBI field office. Grace Sheehan was Chief of the Behavior Analysis Unit at the Boston field office, and not someone Kelly was personally acquainted with. "What about McDonald?"

"He's good, but Grace owes me one. Tell her I asked specifically for her to look at the case."

"Okay. I'll take care of it today."

"Good. I gotta run."

The line went dead, but Kelly held on to the receiver while he spun his Rolodex. He could put all the information on his computer, but he knew where everything was on this antiquated card file, and

136

stubbornly refused to give it up. Quickly finding the number, he punched it in.

"FBI, Boston office."

"Yes, Agent Sheehan, please."

"One moment."

There were several clicks as the call moved through various trackers and recorders. "Behavioral Analysis."

"Agent Sheehan, please."

"This is Sheehan."

"Agent Sheehan, this is Lieutenant Marcus Kelly from BPD precinct C-6."

"Afternoon, Lieutenant. How can I help you?"

"We have a case over here that might benefit from your unit's expertise. Captain Walsh suggested I give you a call."

"Walsh is good people. What's the basics?"

"Two female bodies, close proximity dump sites, same injuries, same basic physical description."

"Interesting. I can come by tomorrow morning. Will the detectives handling the case be there?"

"Give me a time and I'll make sure they are."

"Okay, how about nine?"

"Perfect. See you then, and thanks."

He hung up the phone and punched in another number.

"This is Murphy."

"Murph, it's Kelly."

"Yeah, boss?"

"Need you here by nine tomorrow morning. BAU is sending an analyst over."

"Oh... okay. Can do."

"Alert Sullivan for me, will ya?"

"Yes, sir."

Kelly hung up again. Taking out his cellphone, he hit redial. Within seconds, he was leaving his fourth message of the afternoon.

WEDNESDAY, NOVEMBER 10

PRECINCT C-6
8:30 A.M.

The autopsy and forensic reports were on their desks when the two detectives arrived at the precinct the next day. Neither report did anything to shed light on what direction to take with the two cases.

Danny was sipping his second cup of coffee, staring at crime scene photos for the tenth time that morning, when he noticed a petite, dark-haired woman come into the squad room. She went directly to Lieutenant Kelly's office.

Danny rolled back to where Murphy could hear him. "Looks like our profiler is here."

Murphy nodded as he hung up his phone. "Yeah. You got the Brennan case file?"

"Right here."

"Okay. I've got Nolan's. Let's go."

As they walked toward the conference room in the far corner, the lieutenant and his guest came out of his office and headed for the same place. They filed in together,

139

taking seats on opposite sides of the long table. The detectives on one side, the lieutenant and agent on the other.

The conference room was sparse, with only one exterior window and a large whiteboard on the brick end wall. The interior walls facing the squad room were sound-deadening glass, and six tattered chairs surrounded the table, reflecting hours of discussions and years of meetings.

Kelly was the last to be seated after closing the door. "Agent Sheehan, this is Detective Murphy, and his partner, Detective Sullivan."

Sheehan stood and shook both detectives' hands, surprising Danny with her grip, strong for such a petite woman. Her dark hair was matched by dark, intense eyes, but her smile was quick and disarming. "Nice to meet you, gentlemen."

She returned to her seat and opened a portfolio that contained a legal pad. Writing the date and time across the top, she noted both detectives' names. Finally, she clicked her pen and sat back in her chair, her back straight, her expression serious.

Kelly looked at the two file folders, one in front of each of his detectives. "Which one has Brennan?"

Danny flipped opened the cover on his folder. "I do."

"Okay, give us a rundown."

Danny spent the next ten minutes going over what they knew about the death of Cary Brennan. Sheehan didn't interrupt once, but did make several notes. When he was done, Kelly looked at the agent. "Questions?"

She shook her head. "Not yet."

"Okay Murph, you're up."

Murphy went slightly longer than his partner, in part because there were differences with the autopsy, but Sheehan never stopped him. By the time Murphy finished, the agent's pad was covered with notes.

She stood and started to pace the room. "Forgive me, gentlemen, but I like to think on my feet."

After a couple trips back and forth along the glass wall, she stopped, turning to Danny. "How was victim one subdued? Any Taser burns on her?"

"We're waiting to hear. They weren't found at autopsy, but they may have been concealed by bruising. The coroner is re-examining the photos."

Sheehan nodded and went to her notes, jotting something down. Her pacing restarted. "Did victim two's cellphone reveal anything?"

Murphy cleared his throat. "No. Just calls to a few numbers, none of which couldn't be explained as normal interactions."

"And there were no hairs or fibers found at either scene?"

Murphy shook his head.

More pacing. "What about the boat shoe? Either victim have a connection to the water or boating?"

Danny realized they hadn't exhausted that avenue, but Murphy answered. "Not that we've found to this point."

The agent stopped to make a few more notes before resuming her back and forth. "What about the location? Have you looked for a connection between the victims and the JFK Library?"

That was something Danny hadn't even considered, but again, Murphy answered. "Haven't found anything. I was going on the idea that this particular area was comfortable for the killer."

Sheehan smiled for the first time since the introductions. "Usually, that's the case." She turned to Kelly. "I think I've got enough. You'll send copies of the files to my office?"

The lieutenant stood. "They'll get it done as soon as we're finished here."

"Good. I'll try to have something for you in twenty-four to thirty-six hours."

142

John C. Dalglish

Kelly opened the door, and Sheehan gathered up her notes, stopping to thank the detectives. When Kelly and Sheehan had left, Danny smiled at Murphy. "Impressive."

Murphy's face remained serious. "Indeed. Come on, we have files to copy."

At his desk, Murphy found a file folder and showed it to Danny. "From Megan Quinn."

He flipped it open to find a photo with two red circles drawn on it, which highlighted a faded mark and a bruised area. Written in the same red marker, the words *Suspicious marks, likely Taser burns.* Arrows pointed from the writing to the two circles.

Murphy pulled loose a note attached to the back of the photo. He read it aloud to Danny.

"Detective, I can't be one hundred percent certain, but I believe these spots could be Taser marks. The bruising and blood pooling make it difficult to be sure."

He handed the note to Danny. "I'm sure Miss Sheehan will be very interested to hear that."

LIEUTENANT KELLY'S OFFICE
1:15 P.M.

After having lunch at Mul's, the two detectives returned to find notes on their desks. The lieutenant wanted to see them both when they got back. They'd each grabbed a file and headed to the office. Kelly seemed to Danny to be exceptionally tense.

The lieutenant looked from one detective to the other. "Okay, I heard what you gave Agent Sheehan, but now I want to hear what you have in the way of suspects."

Again, his head swiveled from one man to the other. Finally, Murphy shrugged. "I'm afraid we don't have a single solid one right now."

Kelly leaned back and put his hands behind his head, staring at the ceiling. "Dang, Murph! That's not good enough."

Murphy's tone had an edge to it. "I'm sorry, Marcus. I can't make something appear out of thin air."

"Well, what is your next step?"

"I figured we would talk to all of Nolan's fellow employees. Maybe someone saw something or owns a gray sedan."

"Makes sense. What about you, Sullivan. Any ideas?"

Danny's pulse quickened, uncomfortable at surprising his partner with a theory he hadn't shared. "Actually, I've been looking into a connection between the cases."

Murphy's head swiveled quickly in Danny's direction. "Have you now?"

Danny went on the defensive immediately. "Yeah. I haven't mentioned it because I wasn't sure it had any merit."

Kelly rocked forward in his chair. "Every theory needs to be fleshed out. What is it?"

"Well..." Danny focused on the lieutenant, ignoring the glare from his partner. "Joe Turner mentioned Cary Brennan had reported a prowler. I ran a search on 10-13 calls, looking for reports filed on prowlers. I found Cary Brennan's, but I also found one by Lisa Nolan. Both women had reported prowlers in the weeks before their murders."

The lieutenant was watching him very carefully, and Danny was sure they were sharing the same thought. *Would he bring up their conversation from the day before?* Danny had no intention of going there.

Kelly sat back. "Interesting. What can we do with it?"

"Well, I ran a similar search for the past two months and found eleven instances."

Kelly's eyebrows shot up. "That seems like alot."

"It is. In the past twelve months, there have only been a total of nineteen."

The lieutenant looked from Danny to Murphy and back again. "What are you suggesting we do with this information?"

"Well, with the uptick over the last two months, I thought we could put the women in the other reports under surveillance. Maybe our killer is stalking them first."

Kelly snorted. "Nine women under surveillance! I don't have those kind of resources, Sullivan."

Danny didn't know what to say, and when he looked at Murphy, it was clear he wasn't getting any help there. "Like I said, I wasn't sure it was a useful idea."

"Actually, it's a good avenue to follow. You just haven't done your homework, yet."

"Homework, sir?"

"You've got nine women, all of whom have one connection with our victims, the 10-13 reports. Now, you need to find another connection, even several if you can, to narrow the possibilities. Do that, and I'll consider your idea further."

"Yes, sir."

"Okay, it looks like you both have work to do. Let's get on it."

Both detectives stood and left the office. When they arrived at their desks, Murphy turned to Danny, blocking his path. His voice was just above a whisper. "Don't *ever* do that to me again, understand?"

Danny nodded, his partner's face just inches from his own. "I hadn't intended it to go like that."

Murphy walked off toward the coffee machine, leaving Danny standing there. Getting away from Murphy for the afternoon seemed an especially good idea, so Danny grabbed his reports and left.

TELEGRAPH HILL
6:45 P.M.

Danny had spoken with six of the nine women from his report. A pattern was beginning to emerge, which was what the lieutenant was hoping for, but each time it was repeated, it sent new chills up Danny's spine.

Five of the six women had dirty-blonde hair and dark eyes. The other woman had brown hair. As he rang the doorbell at house number seven, he heard a voice behind him. "Can I help you?"

Danny turned to see a woman in her mid-forties, with dirty-blonde hair and brown eyes, coming up the walk toward him. "Yes, are you Jennifer Morris?"

"Who's asking?"

Danny revealed the badge around his neck. "Detective Sullivan, Boston PD."

She glanced at the badge, then stepped past him. "Come in, Detective. This wind is brutal."

He followed her into a small foyer. "Thank you."

She set the groceries down on a small bench in hall. "What can I do for you?"

"You reported a prowler about ten days ago, correct?"

"That's right. Did you catch him?"

"I'm afraid not. However, there have been others, and I'm following up on all of them."

"Well, I told the officer everything, which I grant you, wasn't much."

Danny took out his notepad. "Would you go over it once more for me?"

"Well... I was coming back from the bus stop, and sensed I was being followed. When I got inside the house, I left the lights off and checked out the front window. A car went by slowly, and I could see a man looking toward the house, but I didn't get a good look at him."

Danny opened the file he was carrying and looked at the report. "I don't see any notation of a car. Did you tell the officer?"

"Yes. I told him exactly like I just told you."

Danny looked at the officer's name: Jack Duffy. "Could you describe the car for me?"

"He had only the parking lights on, so I didn't see much detail. A light colored, four-door sedan."

Danny scribbled the description. However vaguely, it matched the description he'd gotten from Greg Larson. "Could it have been gray?"

"Yeah, I suppose."

"Have you seen it since?"

"No."

"Okay, thank you for your time." He handed her a card. "Please call if you think of anything else."

"Of course, and you let me know if you catch him."

Danny smiled. "Deal."

Back outside, Danny looked at the next address and headed for his car. Two more to go before he could head home.

BOSTON HOMICIDE

THURSDAY, NOVEMBER 11

LIEUTENANT KELLY'S OFFICE
_8:20 A.M._

Marcus Kelly looked at his desk phone as it rang. His morning was already going badly, and he figured whoever was on that line could only make it worse. He'd finally got a response to all the voicemails he'd left yesterday, but it had come in the form of a text message. He looked at the words for the tenth time.

Stop calling! Don't call me anymore.

She wasn't going to let him get close, not now. He snapped his cellphone shut, anger rising inside until his face started to turn red. Snatching up the still ringing desk phone, he barked into the receiver. "Kelly!"

"Good morning to you, too."

"Sorry, Cap. I guess I'm wound a little tight this morning."

"Something I should know about?"

"No, sir."

"Okay, then do me the honor of an update on the two dead girls from the JFK Library area."

The captain was going to want more than "maybe" or "possibly." Stalling seemed to be the best option. "I'm meeting with Murphy and Sullivan this morning. Let me call you afterward with the latest."

"Fine, but why don't you come by my office instead."

"I'll do that."

"Good."

The line went dead and Marcus hung up the phone.

He opened his cellphone and read the message again. He considered whether to call his lawyer and attempt to arrange a meeting with her through the proper channels, but thought better of it. He wasn't in the mood for diplomacy.

Danny had made a point to be in early that morning, much to the frustration of Cassie, who was getting tired of being pregnant alone.

"I'm starting to feel like a single mother-to-be!"

"Come on Cass, don't be like that. You know I don't have a choice when I'm in the middle of a case."

She had refused to look at him, instead focusing on the load of laundry she was sorting. "I miss you."

"And I miss you. As soon as I have my wits about me, the new job will settle down."

"I hope so."

"Besides, the money will help alot with the new baby."

She had shrugged, seemingly unmoved by his reasoning. Nevertheless, he wanted to make sure he had a chance to patch things up with Murphy. All the notes from his previous night's canvassing were laid out and ready to be reviewed by his partner.

Just finishing his second cup of coffee, he spotted Murphy coming through the squad room door. Murphy nodded at him and sat down, pulling out his own notepad. Danny rolled his chair across the aisle. "Hey, Murph."

"Yeah?"

"I didn't get a chance to say sorry for screwing up yesterday. I shouldn't have let it go down like it did."

"Forget it."

"Yeah... okay. Mind if I get your opinion on what I learned last night?"

Murphy turned around and stood up, going to Danny's desk. "What have you got?"

Danny briefed him on everything, including his conclusions. Murphy nodded several times, mumbled something about not being sure what they could do with the information, before returning to his desk.

Danny figured he's done his best to make sure his partner wasn't blindsided again, whether he appreciated it or not, but Murphy surprised him by coming back to his desk carrying his own notepad. "I interviewed everyone I could find at Shenannigans', but only one person drove a gray sedan. She's a single mother without an alibi, so I had to arrest her."

Danny looked up in surprise. "Arrest her?"

Murphy was grinning at him. Danny heaved a sigh of relief. "You're a funny guy, Murph! A funny guy!"

"Murphy, Sullivan! Got a minute?"

The detectives turned to see the lieutenant signaling them. Murphy grunted. "Seems we're in demand."

They each loaded up their notes and went into Kelly's office. Murphy shut the door behind them. "Morning, Lieutenant."

"Good morning, Murph, Sullivan. The captain is rattling his sabre. What have you guys got for me?"

Murphy shook his head slowly. "I'm afraid I came up empty last night, but I think the kid may have something."

The lieutenant's head swiveled in Danny's direction. "Good. Let's hear it."

Danny slipped two sheets of paper out of his folder, handing one to Murphy and sliding the other across the desk toward the lieutenant. "Sir, I spoke to all nine of the women who had also reported a prowler in the last two months... "

"All nine?"

"Yes, sir. I was very fortunate."

"I'll say."

Murphy laughed. "So that's what they call beginner's luck!"

Danny smiled sheepishly and shrugged, then pushed on, gesturing at the notes. "As you can see, all of them have dirty-blonde to brown hair. In addition, they all have dark eyes and are roughly the same height."

"While this gives us a definite profile of who our perp likes, it doesn't narrow it down any."

"Yes, sir, I realize that." Danny pulled out another pair of sheets, repeating the hand out process. "This particular woman,

Jennifer Morris, is different from the others in two respects."

Kelly lifted a single eyebrow. "Really? How so?"

"First of all, she's the only one in her mid-forties, forty-four to be specific, which matches our victims."

"Okay, and second?"

"She was followed by a light-colored sedan. She said it *could* have been gray, but she wasn't certain."

"Those are significant, but I can't do open-ended surveillance without knowing the goal."

Murphy cleared his throat. "I may have something on that. Both victims disappeared during the Sunday night to Monday morning time frame. Suppose we do stakeouts during the weekends, specifically from Friday night to Monday morning?"

Danny hadn't picked up on that detail, but it made sense. Both detectives now watched their lieutenant for a reaction. After several minutes, Kelly stood. "You guys stay nearby. I'm gonna take this up to Captain Walsh."

"Yes, sir."

CAPTAIN WALSH'S OFFICE
9:30 A.M.

"Marcus, come in."

Kelly entered the office and closed the door behind him. He tossed the two sheets of paper from his detective onto the captain's desk.

Walsh looked at them then at his lieutenant. "What are those?"

"They were given to me by Sullivan. He's been doing some checking into prowler reports in Southie, something both our victims had filed. He's come up with a possible profile for our killer's targets, and a suggestion for catching him."

Walsh picked up the papers and scanned them. "Interesting."

Kelly shrugged. "Might be something, might not be."

"What does he propose we do with the information?"

"He and Murphy think doing weekend surveillance of the Morris woman might flush our killer."

"And what do you think?"

Kelly shrugged again. "It's something, at least. Right now, we're pissing into the wind."

Walsh looked at the sheets again, then slid them back to his lieutenant. "I like it. Especially because it's being proactive, and I can tell the chief we're moving forward."

Kelly sighed and retrieved the sheets, heading for the door. "Okay, Cap. Consider it a go."

Before he could open the door, Walsh stopped him. "Marcus?"

"Yeah?"

"You sure everything is okay?"

"Yeah, it's good... I'm good."

"Things any better with Maria?"

Kelly didn't like the prying, and he wasn't about to hash it out with his boss. "Some."

The captain studied his lieutenant, then smiled. "Tell the men I said nice work and good luck."

"Yes, sir."

Kelly left the office and took the elevator down to the squad room. When the doors opened, he spotted Sullivan and Murphy leaning over Sullivan's desk. He walked up behind them. "Gentlemen."

"Sir?"

"The captain likes your idea. He's green-lighted it, so get with Miss Morris, pick your locations, and give me a briefing in the morning."

"Yes, sir."

FRIDAY, NOVEMBER 12

PARKING LOT
PRECINCT C-6
7:50 A.M.

Danny parked his car just as the first snow of the season started to fall. There was very little wind, so it came down with an eerie silence, slowly covering the world in white. He was about to swing his door open when a black, two-door sedan pulled in next to him and forced him to stop. The vehicle was close enough to prevent him from getting out comfortably, and he was about to get angry, when he heard the whirring of the passenger window being lowered.

At first, all Danny could make out was black curly hair and deep brown eyes. They were quickly followed by a wide white smile and a feminine voice. "Detective Sullivan, right?"

"Yeah."

"I was hoping to catch you this morning."

As his eyes adjusted to the darkness in the stranger's car, her smooth dark skin was revealed. "Looks like it's your lucky day. Who are you?"

"Lieutenant Jan Michaels."

"What's your interest in talking to me?"

"You're Raymond Murphy's new partner, aren't you?"

Danny suddenly had a very uneasy feeling. "What division did you say you're with?"

"I didn't. I'm with BPD Internal Affairs."

Danny closed his door and slid across the front seat to get out on the other side. He locked his car and headed for the precinct doors.

"Detective Sullivan, stop!"

He had no choice but to obey the order of a superior. He froze in place without turning around. The snow muffled her footsteps approaching rapidly from behind, and when she moved around in front of him, he was mildly surprised to find her nearly a foot shorter than him. This apparently didn't bother her, because she stood very close and looked up into his face.

"I'm going to tell you three things. One—Detective Murphy has a checkered past when it comes to playing by the rules. Two—as his partner, you need to be careful you don't pick up any of his questionable habits..."

Danny continued to stare straight ahead, his gaze carrying over her head, toward the parking lot beyond. His main concern was not being seen with an IA investigator.

"... Third, if you ever see something, hear something, heck even smell something is not right with Murphy, you bring it to me." She stuck a business card in his top pocket. "If things hit the fan, I might be your only friend."

Danny shifted his gaze down to her. Their eyes met for an instant, then she stepped aside. Danny continued on toward the precinct, and when he looked back from the front door of the building, Lieutenant Michaels was gone.

While waiting for the elevator, he pulled out the card and stared at it.

It had been drilled into him since he was old enough to understand what Internal Affairs was, you don't talk to the "rat squad", especially if you didn't want to be shunned by your fellow officers. His reaction to Michaels had almost been instinctive.

He studied the card for another moment, tempted to throw it in the trash, but didn't. Instead, he put it back in his pocket.

What does that say about your feelings for your partner, Danny-boy?

It was a question that didn't need an answer.

MAJOR CASE
CONFERENCE ROOM
9:02 A.M.

Murphy and Sullivan filed into the meeting room to find the lieutenant and a second man, who Danny instantly recognized. "Sergeant Buckley, nice to see you."

The big man with flaming red hair and huge hands shook with Danny, visibly vibrating the young detective with the force of his handshake. "Danny-boy, good to see you. I didn't know this was your gig I was asked to sit in on."

"Mine and Murphy's. You know Ray Murphy, don't you."

"Sure, sure." They shook hands. "Good to see you, Detective."

Danny sensed a coolness between the two men, but wasn't sure if it was real or just the events in the parking lot toying with his imagination.

Once everyone was seated, Lieutenant Kelly brought things around to the topic at hand. "What did you guys accomplish yesterday?"

Murphy looked at Danny and nodded. Danny unfolded a map of the Southie area and marked the location of Jennifer Morris's home, then the bus stop she used, and finally, the place they'd decided to utilize as their stakeout point. "This location gives us a view of the front of her home, the street as she comes down from the bus stop, and the alley behind her place."

Buckley frowned. "What about the stop itself? You can't see it from there."

"True, and we're hoping to get a little help with that."

The sergeant nodded. "I can have an officer watch it *if* I have a man available."

"I can give you a small window, roughly a half hour, that we need someone there."

Buckley nodded. "Like I said, *if* I have a free officer."

Kelly looked at Danny, then to Murphy. "What if he doesn't have a free man?"

Murphy pointed at their stakeout spot, then ran his finger along the map to the bus stop. "The distance is only two blocks. One of us will walk up to make a visual, staying out of sight until after Jennifer has passed us."

"And you start this tonight?"

Both detectives nodded.

"Good. I'll let the captain know."

A knock at the door rotated all heads in that direction. Agent Grace Sheehan stuck her head through the crack in the door. "Got a minute, Gentlemen?"

Kelly waved at her. "Of course. Come in."

Buckley stood. "You can have my chair, I've got to run."

The lieutenant and sergeant shook hands. "Thanks, Sergeant."

"No problem."

When the door was closed again, the BAU analyst handed out three files, keeping a fourth for herself. Danny opened his to find two neatly typed pages on FBI letterhead. The first was titled *SUSPECT PROFILE* and the second, *CRIMINAL CHARACTERISTICS*.

Sheehan didn't sit at the table, but instead went to the whiteboard at the end of the room and picked up a marker. "You can read it all for yourself later, but here are the key points."

She wrote as she talked. "One—our guy is likely between thirty-five and forty-five, and fairly fit. Because of the use of a Taser, he would have to be able to lift, or at least support, the victims into his vehicle himself. Second—he has a means of getting close enough to use the Taser, so either the victims know him, or perhaps he has some sort of an official ID. It's possible that both apply, but it's possible neither apply."

She turned and looked at the two detectives. "As you know, this is not an exact science."

They nodded and she returned to the board. "Third—the lack of a sexual angle, and the posing of the body, suggest a personal vendetta. It could be anger at women in general, problems with a particular woman, or maybe some individual aspect of the women he chooses. Regardless, he is unlikely to break from the pattern, and therefore similar characteristics should be a red flag for anyone he might target."

Danny saw the logic in all of it, and felt they were on the right path with Jennifer Morris. Sheehan's final point was unsettling.

"Finally, the distinct cleanliness of the crime scene speaks to someone with experience in such things. A cop, doctor, clinical worker, hospital worker, or possibly a lab tech."

She set the marker down and turned to the room. "Any questions?"

Murphy closed his file folder. "Just one. Do you have any suggestion about what kind of weapon our man is using?"

The profiler shook her head. "I'm afraid nothing in particular, but it's likely a tool of whatever trade the killer belongs to."

She looked from Murphy to Danny, and then to the lieutenant. "If that's all, then I have to run."

Kelly stood. "Thanks a bunch, Grace."

"Anytime. Good luck, Detectives."

When she was gone, Kelly turned to the two detectives. "Okay. Looks like you've got some reading material. Take it home with you, go over it, grab some shut-eye, and be back for the detail at nine tonight."

He left, and the two detectives gathered up their papers before heading for the door. Danny was now front and center. The stakeout was his idea, and his stock would rise or fall based on how it went. His stomach was slightly queasy as he stepped out into the now snow-covered parking lot. A quick scan of the lot gave him some relief.

At least there's no sign of the IA investigator.

SULLIVAN RESIDENCE
WEST ROXBURY
8:20 P.M.

Danny had just finished dinner and was preparing to leave for the first night's surveillance. Cassie was unusually quiet, and the tension between them was thick, but Danny didn't see where he had any choice.

"Cass?"

She didn't turn around from the dishes she was doing, nor did she answer him. He got up and went to her, kissing her neck, then rubbing her shoulders. "You okay?"

She shrugged while drying her hands.

Danny turned her toward him and was heartbroken to see dried tears on her face. "Cass, don't cry. It's just for a couple nights."

She looked up at him, their nearly full-term baby filling the space between them. Her tears restarted, rolling down her face. "I didn't know..."

He steered her toward the couch and sat down next to her. "What are you talking about? What didn't you know?"

"That it would be like this."

Danny tried not to become impatient. "What would?"

She pawed at her face, trying to brush away the tears. "You being a detective!"

Danny stared at her, surprise evident on his face. Like a dam that had been breached, she poured out her feelings.

"I was so proud of you, I *am* proud of you, but..."

He brushed a lock of hair out of her eyes. "But?"

"Well, I thought it would be great. More money, regular hours, and not having to worry about you on patrol, but it hasn't been that way at all. You're never home. Your work schedule varies according to the status of the case you're on. I... miss you."

Unsure what to do, he pulled her close. "It won't always be like..."

She pushed back from him, her eyes flaring with a mixture of pain and anger. "You can't say that! You don't know if it will change or not, in fact, you probably realize it won't."

He stared at her in silence.

Was this the pregnancy talking or something else? Had he misjudged her enthusiasm for the promotion? Was he the one who wanted it, not her, and it was all about him being the first detective in the family?

168

The moment was broken by the phone ringing. Cass looked at it with disgust. "You have to go. I'll be fine."

Danny answered it. "Hello?"

"Oh, Danny! Thank the sweet Lord you're home."

"Mom? What is it?"

"Your father is in an ambulance... and you need to get to the hospital... and I need to call your brother and sister... and I can't believe..."

"Mom! Slow down!" Danny looked over at Cass, who was watching him, her own tears forgotten. "Tell me what happened, slowly."

He could hear his mother take a big breath, trying to calm herself. Her voice had come down about three octaves when she re-started. "Your father had a heart attack, at least that's what the medics said. He's on his way to Boston Medical Center."

Fear raced around his entire body as adrenaline pumped through him. "Is he going to be okay?"

"I don't know. They worked on him, then loaded him into the ambulance. They asked me if I wanted to go with them but I needed to get dressed." Her voice started to rise again.

"Okay, Mom... Listen to me."

"I don't know what to do."

"Mom? Mom! Listen."

"Okay...Okay, I'm listening."

"Cass and I will pick you up in twenty minutes. Don't call Sean or Bree until we find out exactly what the situation is, then *I* will call them. Okay?"

"Okay."

"Get dressed; we're on our way."

Danny hung up and gave Cass the thirty-second rundown. They both grabbed their coats and headed out the door, grateful the snow had stopped. They didn't need any delays tonight.

BOSTON MEDICAL CENTER
SOUTH BOSTON
9:45 P.M.

Danny, Cass, and Aileen found Patrick Sullivan in the emergency department, sitting up in bed. He smiled at them when they arrived, but the grin did nothing to conceal the effect of what he'd just gone through. "Hey, everyone."

Aileen rushed to his side and wrapped herself around his neck. "Are you going to die?"

He gently pried her loose. "No, Mother, I'm not going to die."

His father's appearance left Danny unsettled. He was pale and his skin was drawn. Danny couldn't remember seeing his father ever look so old. "What did the doctor say?"

"He called it a coronary artery spasm."

"Which is?"

"Apparently it's a type of attack that may come and go. He said it's treated with medications."

"Can you go home tonight?"

His father shook his head. "He wants me to stay overnight for observation and a few more tests."

Danny's phone started to ring. He stepped out into the hallway before answering. "Sullivan."

"Where are you?"

"What... or crap, Murph. I totally forgot to call."

"Why would you be calling? You're supposed to be here for the surveillance, the one *you* suggested!"

"Yeah, I know. It's my pop; he's had a heart attack."

"Oh... I'm sorry. Is he okay?"

"He will be. I'm at the hospital now, but I'll be there shortly."

"Don't be ridiculous. I'll take the watch tonight and you stay with your pop."

"Thanks, Murph. You'll tell the lieutenant?"

"Yeah. Talk to you tomorrow."

Danny hung up, and figured it was time to call his siblings. He stepped into the nearby stairwell and dialed Sean first.

SATURDAY, NOVEMBER 13

BOSTON MEDICAL CENTER
SOUTH BOSTON
_9:05 A.M._

Danny had tried to persuade his mother to go home for the night, but to no avail, and she'd spent the night in a chair next to her husband. He found both of them awake, his father looking much better than he had the night before.

Walking over to his mother, he kissed her on the top of the head, then laid his hand on his father's arm. "How you feelin', Pop?"

"Better, except I'm starving. There's none of your mother's good Irish cooking here."

"Knock, knock."

Everyone turned to see Kevin Doyle standing in the doorway. Danny smiled at his friend. "Hey, Kev."

"Hi, Danny. Hey Mr. Sullivan, Mrs. Sullivan."

Aileen stood and moved toward the door. "Nice to see you, Kevin. I'll leave you boys to talk while I go in search of a good cup of coffee."

After she'd left, Kevin came into the room. "I heard about the ticker, Mr. Sullivan. Everything going to be okay?"

"Sure, sure. I'm gonna be fine. What have you been up to?"

"Oh, you know. On duty, off duty, on duty."

The elder Sullivan laughed. "I used to know, but that's another story."

Danny was leaning against the window, watching the exchange. "How'd you hear, Kev?"

"Murphy. Buckley had me watch the bus stop last night, and I talked to Murph afterward."

Pat grinned at the mention of an old friend. " Buckley is a good man."

"Yeah. Well, I just wanted to check on you, sir."

"I appreciate it."

Kevin appeared ready to go. "Got a minute, Danny?"

"Sure. Back in a few, Pop."

"Take your time."

The two friends headed out into the hall and toward the elevator. Danny patted his friend on the shoulder. "It was real good of you to come by."

Kevin shrugged. "It was nothing. So, you gonna be on detail tonight?"

"Yeah, I think so."

"Cool. Maybe we'll get a chance to grab a coffee. So, why did you decide to watch this particular woman?"

"She fit a profile we came up with from the first two victims."

"Got any leads on the killer?"

"Not yet. We did receive some help from the BAU."

"Oh, yeah? What kind of help?"

"They gave us a profile of the killer to work with."

Kevin shifted from one leg to the other. "Anybody I know?"

Danny laughed. "Oh, I see how it is. You want in on the bust!"

Kevin grinned. "Something like that."

The elevator arrived and the doors opened. Kevin stepped in and Danny shook his hand. "Don't worry, Kev. You'll get your shot at detective."

CITY POINT NEIGHBORHOOD
7:50 P.M.

Marcus Kelly pulled down Swallow Street and parked across from a three-story, row-house duplex. One half was covered with gray siding, and the other with beige. It was a common sight in Southie, a way for

175

people to say "this half is mine." His interest was on the gray side, and he sat nervously watching the front door.

If he had his timing right, she would be coming out any moment. His timing was perfect.

"Hey!"

The woman's reaction was instant and angry. "What are you doing here? You can't be here!"

Kelly started to get out of his car. "Please, I just want to talk to you."

"Stay back. You know you're violating the protection order!" She reached in her purse and pulled out her phone. "If you get out of that car, I'm calling 9-1-1."

"Will you just listen for a moment?"

She started toward her car. "There's nothing I want to hear from you."

"Look, I promise it will never happen again."

She climbed into her car, slammed the door, and drove off. Kelly shut his own door, looked around to see if anyone was watching, then pulled away from the curb.

PRECINCT C-6
9:15 P.M.

Danny sat at his desk, anxious to get going, but Murphy hadn't shown yet. Lost in his thoughts, he was startled when the phone rang. "Sullivan."

"Hey, it's Murph. I won't make detail tonight."

"Okay... What's up?"

"I'm not sure. I think I have a bug."

"No problem, I'll handle it. I owe you anyway."

"Thanks. Is the lieutenant still hanging around?"

"No, I haven't seen him."

"Okay, I'll let him know. Good luck tonight."

"Thanks, Murph. Feel better."

Danny hung up and headed for the parking lot. He'd done some surveillance when he was in patrol, mostly as a backup, but he was about to do his first full-blown stakeout.

Don't forget the coffee thermos!

He shook it and smiled to himself.

You've already drank most of it, better stop for a refill.

Dunkin' Donuts just became a priority-one stop along the way.

TELEGRAPH HILL
11:30 P.M.

Danny had gone through half of his coffee and most of the donuts. He was quickly becoming aware of what stakeout pounds were, based on how much he'd eaten. He picked up his radio and called in.

"Sullivan to Dispatch."

"Go ahead, Detective."

"Patch me through to Sergeant Buckley, please."

"One moment."

Danny sat eyeballing another donut while he waited, finally deciding to close the top of the box. "This is Buckley."

"Hey, Sergeant. This Danny Sullivan. Can you spare a man to watch the bus stop?"

"Sorry, Danny. I don't have anyone tonight. Typical Saturday. If Doyle gets free from his 10-13, I'll have him get over there, but I can't promise anything."

Danny pushed himself up in his seat. "Did you say 10-13?"

"Yeah, over in the City Point area."

"Kevin Doyle is the responding officer?"

"Yeah, why?"

"Just curious. Don't worry about my detail, I can handle it. Have Kevin give me a call when he's done, will ya?"

"Sure thing. Buckley out."

Danny was getting that eerie feeling again, and he didn't like it one bit.

He climbed out of his car and walked up to where he could get a visual on the bus stop. There were light snow flurries falling but very little wind, which helped keep the cold at bay while he was outside.

Within fifteen minutes, he spotted Jennifer Morris getting off the bus. She looked around, probably trying to spot the surveillance, before coming down the street toward Danny's position. He waited for her to pass by, before continuing down to his car.

She turned around when she heard his footsteps, but Danny could see the recognition on her face, and she kept up her pace toward her front door. Danny climbed back in his car and watched her disappear into the house.

He would stay another half hour before calling it a night.

****

Danny was on his way home when his phone rang. "Sullivan."

"Hey, Danny. Sergeant said you wanted me to call."

"Yeah. I was curious about the 10-13 you were on tonight."

"What about it?"

"Did you find the prowler?"

"No, he was long gone."

"Who was the victim?"

"Uh... Sandra Cooper. Why?"

Danny got the distinct impression Kevin would rather not talk about it. "Could you describe her to me?"

"Well... let's see. Tall, mid-forties, blonde, big smile."

"Interesting. Did you file your report yet?"

"Nah. I'll do it when I get back to the station."

"Okay. Thanks for calling, buddy."

"Sure thing."

The line went dead. Danny now had another name to add to his prowler list.

SUNDAY, NOVEMBER 14

HOME OF
PATRICK & AILEEN SULLIVAN
11:55 A.M.

When Danny and Cass arrived at his parent's home in Southie, they found Pat Sullivan in extremely good spirits. He was sitting up on the couch, a bowl of something Aileen had fixed him in his lap, and smiling broadly. "Danny, Cass! Come in!"

Cass gave her father-in-law a hug. "You're looking good."

"No doubt. The hospital may save your life but it's no place to get better. Home is for that. How are you feeling?"

"Like a balloon in search of a needle!"

Pat laughed with gusto, and Danny felt much better seeing his father's mood. "Hey, Pop."

"Hi, Son. Thanks for taking care of your mother, and calling your brother and sister."

"Of course. Where's mom?"

"Cooking up some more food in the kitchen."

Cass had perched herself on the couch next to her father-in-law, so Danny went in search of his mom. He found her stirring one of the three pots on the stove. He kissed her cheek. "Hey."

"Daniel. I'm glad you could come by today."

"I wanted to check on pop as well as get Cass out of the house."

"Do you have the whole day off?"

"Unfortunately, no. I've got surveillance duty later tonight."

She stopped stirring and studied her son. "I'm going to tell you something, but you must never let your father find out you know, nor that I told you."

"Sure. What is it?"

She looked over his shoulder to make sure no one had come up behind them. "There's a reason your father never made detective."

"Oh?"

"It had nothing to do with whether or not he was qualified."

"What then?"

"He never applied for the job... because of me."

Danny stared at her, surprised such a secret had never come out. "What do you mean 'because of you'?"

She checked over his shoulder again. "Well, actually, it was because of us. Your father didn't want to be away from his family as much as making detective would have required."

Danny was stunned. Cassie's words from the other night came rushing back. "Have you been talking to Cassie?"

His mother had gone back to stirring. "I don't need to talk to her; I can see it on her face. She misses you very much."

"What about Grandpa Francis? Did he try for detective?"

She shrugged. "You'll have to ask him yourself."

Danny's head spun.

Was I the first in the family to make detective because I was the first to apply? Did I miss something along the way that was telling me to make a different choice? Didn't Cass encourage me in the beginning?

His mother was watching him. "Don't take it the wrong way, it wasn't a bad choice you made, and I'm sure Cassie was on board in the beginning. Just don't be surprised if the baby might have changed her point of view."

Danny smiled down at his mother. She never failed to surprise him with her wisdom. "You're an incredible woman, Aileen Sullivan."

She gave him a knowing smile. "Keep that to yourself, okay.

Danny laughed and walked back around the corner to watch Cassie interact with his father. She was the sun in his sky, and he would never want her to be unhappy. He went to the couch and sat next to her, taking her hand as they watched the kickoff of the Patriots game.

TELEGRAPH HILL
11:59 P.M.

Jennifer Morris had just disappeared into her front door, and Danny was feeling dejected. "I thought sure we'd get some sort of an angle on our killer by watching her. Everything pointed to her being next."

Murphy sipped the last of his coffee and smiled at his young partner. "Sometimes it's like that... until it's not."

"Well, at least we get to sleep in tomorrow."

"Yeah. You got any plans?"

Danny laughed. "Not unless Cass goes into labor."

"That's right, she's due isn't she?"

"Technically, she's due on Thanksgiving, but she doesn't look like she'll make it that long."

184

"Babies have their own timetable, that's for sure."

"What about you, Murph. Plans?"

"Not really. Just gonna tie up some loose ends. By the way, if you see your dad, give him my best."

"I will. Should we call it a night?"

"Sounds good to me. I need to unload some of this coffee, anyway."

****

When Murphy dropped him at the precinct, Danny went inside to his desk, and grabbed the folder given them by Grace Sheehan. He sensed he was missing something important, and tomorrow would be a good day to review the file while away from the station.

That was providing Cassie didn't take exception and go into labor

BOSTON HOMICIDE

MONDAY, NOVEMBER 15

SULLIVAN RESIDENCE
WEST ROXBURY
_7:30 A.M._

Despite getting in late, Danny was first up in the morning. Scrambled eggs with salsa, and toast with butter were on the menu, mostly because they seemed to be the only things Cass wanted these days. He was just putting it on the table when she made her way out of the bedroom. "Hungry?"

"Yes and no."

He smiled and kissed her cheek. "I can sympathize, but I'm sure I can't understand."

She picked up her plate and went to the couch, more comfortable in her advanced stage of roundness. Danny got himself some coffee and a glass of juice for Cass, following her to the living room.

They enjoyed the quiet and nearness of each other while they ate. Cass would pause in between bites to lay her hand on his knee. This ritual had become increasingly rare since his new job began. She finished and put her plate on the coffee table. "Thanks."

187

She laid her head against his arm as he sipped his coffee. "You're welcome."

He played with her hair while she closed her eyes, and let his mind wander to the day she surprised him with the news they were going to have a baby. He'd been on the day shift and dinner was ready for him when he got home.

"Perfect timing, I just pulled the lamb out of the oven."

Lamb with mint jelly was one of Danny's favorites. "Awesome."

He kissed her and went to change. When he came out of the bedroom, the table was set with lit candles and she was sitting waiting for him. He grinned at her. "What's all this?"

"All what?"

"Hmmm. Okay, I'll play along."

He sat down and they ate, making small talk. Cassie had managed to act too normal, too casual, and it was freaking him out. When the meal was done, she took the lamb to the kitchen, then stuck her head back around the corner. "Dessert?"

Even though he'd stuffed himself, he knew better than to say no to one of Cassie's desserts. They were her claim to fame in the family. "Of course."

188

She went back in the kitchen, returning in a few minutes with a serving tray, the contents hidden beneath a cover. "This is a new dessert. I hope you like it."

She set the tray down and lifted the cover. Danny found himself staring at four little Gerber baby food jars. "What's this?"

"Peaches, pears, bananas, and apples."

"But... why... It's baby food."

"Oh, didn't I tell you? We're expecting."

Danny was still a little startled. "Expecting?"

"A baby, silly."

Next thing Danny could remember was holding Cass and crying. She produced two baby spoons, a blue spoon for him and a pink for her. They proceeded to laugh their way through two of the jars each, spitting some of the food out, which produced even more fits of laughter.

It was one of Danny's fondest memories. He pulled a lock of hair away from her eyes. "You want me to run you a bath?"

"That sounds wonderful."

He rose from the couch and headed for the bathroom. "Consider it done."

BOSTON HOMICIDE

****

Twenty minutes later, Cassie was soaking in a warm tub. Danny cleaned up the kitchen, then remembered the file he'd brought home. He poured himself another coffee and went to the couch, folder in hand.

After going through the profile again, he set it aside and tried to get a handle on the uneasy feeling he had. The lack of suspects that even remotely fit the profile was troubling. In fact, the complete lack of a solid person of interest was frustrating. But there was something else.

The killings, as well as the prowler incidents, were too clean, too free of mistakes or evidence. Even though he was inexperienced, Danny knew very few crime scenes were completely devoid of anything. The only lead was a shoe print. And maybe that was the reason for his unease.

The words of Grace Sheehan came back to him, still causing the same unsettling reaction.

"Finally, the distinct cleanliness of the crime scene speaks to someone with experience in such things. A cop, doctor, clinical worker, hospital worker, or possibly a lab tech."

They'd come up empty on the idea of a hospital employee, and neither of the victims had any connection to a lab or clinic. That meant, if the profile was accurate, they might be looking for one of their own.

Danny closed his eyes and tried to decide if he wanted to go down that path. It was filled with hidden dangers, some of which could end his career, and was not something encouraged by the rest of the force. Accusing a fellow officer was tantamount to joining IA.

Despite his reservations, his mind began to wander through some of the case's details that fit the cop scenario.

Prowler gone before police arrive, no physical evidence except one shoe print, no forensic evidence, use of high quality plastic handcuffs, a unidentifiable weapon of choice, a disarming persona for the use of a close-contact Taser.

It meant only one thing to Danny, but then it might mean something completely different to a more experienced cop.

A more experienced cop. Like Pat Sullivan.

"Danny!"

He got up and went into the bathroom. Cass was ready to get out and he helped her gingerly step over the edge of the tub. While she toweled herself, he went and sat on the bed. "What do you feel like doing today?"

"You mean besides having a baby?"

He laughed. "Yeah, besides that."

"I don't know; nothing in particular."

"Want to take a ride over to my parent's with me?"

"I guess. Why?"

"I need to run something from work by my dad."

"Okay, but no stopping at the station. You're mine today, right?"

"Right; no stopping at the station, promise."

"Good, because if you break your promise, you're a dead man!"

By the sound of her voice, he couldn't be sure she was kidding.

Better to not take any chances.

HOME OF
PATRICK & AILEEN SULLIVAN
11:15 A.M.

The wind had changed direction and there was talk of a Nor'easter. Those were never welcome on the Eastern seaboard, especially the kind that brings snow measured in feet, but so far it was still a few days out. Danny knocked, then opened the front door. "Hello?"

Aileen Sullivan stuck her head out of the kitchen. "Come in! Come in!"

Danny swung the door wide for Cass, and they stamped their feet while removing their coats. The house was as warm as ever, something Cassie blamed on old age. *"Haven't you noticed elderly folks always have the heat set at like a hundred?"*

Danny had refused to be drawn in to the conversation, wary that Cassie may throw him under the bus one day. *"Danny mentioned how hot you guys keep it."*

His mother had returned to the kitchen, but Danny didn't see his father. "Where's Pop?"

"Right here."

His father had appeared from the hallway. "Hey, Pop. How you feelin'?"

"Pretty good. The new medicine makes me sleepy, which sucks."

"Better sleepy than dead."

"Is that an old Irish Limerick?"

Danny laughed. "How would it go? There was an old cop who was sleepy but not dead..."

Pat Sullivan dropped down on the couch. "That's it!"

"Whatever." Danny joined him. "Speaking of an old cop, I need a wise person to run something by."

"Okay. I don't exactly have a full calendar, so shoot."

Danny looked up to make sure Cass had gone to the kitchen. "It's about the case I'm on right now."

Danny proceeded to lay out the FBI profile, followed by his own theory. By the time he was done, all humor had left his father's face, replaced by a mixture of intensity and concern. It was the look Danny expected to see, but the reaction wasn't what he'd expected to hear.

"What does your gut tell you?"

Danny had prepared himself for multiple warnings about how dangerous his thought process was. "I don't know... like I said, something doesn't feel right."

"Well, I'll give you the advice you're expecting, first. Treading down this path, if you're wrong, could blow up in your face. It could ruin your future, and cost you your friends."

Danny just nodded, already acutely aware of the consequences.

"Having said that, I think some of your suspicions are well-founded. I'm not saying you're right, but you have to at least

John C. Dalglish

consider the possibility. If you don't, you're not doing your job."

Danny was both gratified and surprised. He'd grown up with his father's "don't cross the blue-line attitude" and so he wasn't sure how to respond.

Pat apparently sensed the confusion. "You want to know why I'm telling you this?"

Danny nodded.

"Because you're a detective. That's different than being a front line officer. You have to find the truth, regardless of where it leads. An officer is a responder, not an investigator. There's a difference in duty and responsibility."

"So, because I'm a detective, it's okay for me to go after another officer?"

"I didn't say that! I said you have a different set of responsibilities. Any officer who knows of illegal activity by a fellow officer isn't doing his duty or honoring his oath if he doesn't report it. But a detective must follow where the evidence takes him."

Danny's head spun with his choices, and his predicament, but he was grateful for his father's advice. "Thanks, Pop."

"Anytime. You know I'm here for you."

"Anybody hungry?"

They looked up to see Cassie putting a tray on the table. Both men jumped up. "Yes!"

TUESDAY, NOVEMBER 16

PRECINCT C-6
7:15 A.M.

Danny arrived early, not because he was anxious to get to work, but because he planned to talk with the lieutenant about his theory. If he could catch Kelly before anyone else arrived, perhaps he could avoid curiosity from Murphy and the others. He didn't want people questioning the reason for his conversation with the lieutenant, especially if it didn't go well.

Unfortunately, Murphy was already in when Danny arrived. "Hey, Murph."

"Morning, Glory. Have a good day off?"

"Yeah. You?"

"Quiet. Had a couple drinks with Marcus, nothing special."

"I didn't know you two were friendly outside of work."

Murphy grunted. "We weren't! But, the lieutenant is going through some personal troubles and he called me to meet him. We went to the L-Street Tavern."

Danny couldn't help himself. "What kind of troubles?"

Murphy cast a sideways glance at his partner. "Keep your mouth shut, okay?"

Danny nodded.

"He and his wife are looking at divorce."

Danny looked toward the office where the lieutenant was already at his desk. "That sucks."

Murphy also looked toward the office. "Yeah. I guess he wanted to talk to someone who'd been through it."

Danny decided to wait until later to bring up the topic weighing on his mind, but fate intervened. "Sullivan!"

"Sir?"

"Got a minute?"

"Yes, sir."

Murphy grabbed his arm as Danny started toward the office. "Not a word."

"I got it, Murph. Promise."

Danny leaned in the office door. "What's up, Lieutenant?"

"Come in; shut the door."

Danny did as the lieutenant asked, leaning against it once it was closed. Kelly waved at the chairs in front of him. "Sit, please."

When Danny was comfortable, Kelly opened a folder. "So, it's been what... two weeks?"

"Sir?"

"Since you made detective."

"Yes, sir."

The phone rang and Kelly answered it, giving Danny a 'hold on a moment' wave. Danny let his gaze travel around the office, looking at nothing in particular, until something began to nag at his subconscious.

There's something different. Something missing, maybe?

He'd been focusing on picking up details around him, something Murphy had mentioned was a good habit to get into, and Danny sensed he was failing at it right now.

What is it? Come on, Danny-boy, figure it out.

He didn't get a chance to finish his self-challenge before Kelly hung up. "Now, where were we? Oh, yes, you've been on the job two weeks." Kelly leaned back in his chair. "How's it going?"

"Good. Be better if we could get a handle on the dead women case."

"No question. Are you comfortable with Murphy? Are you two getting along okay?"

"Yes, sir. No problems."

"Good, good. Do you have any questions for me?"

"You mean in reference to my duties?"

"Exactly."

Danny shook his head. "I think I'm settling in okay."

Kelly rocked forward, making a note in the file, which Danny could now see had his name on it. "Well look, I just needed to do an update to your progress, but you can go ahead and get back to work on those murders."

Danny took a quick look over his shoulder, but didn't see Murphy. "Actually, sir..."

The lieutenant looked up from his notes. "Yes?"

"I'd like to speak to you off the record."

Kelly put down his pen and regarded Danny with an apparent guarded wariness. "Okay...In reference to?"

"The case I'm on with Murphy."

"Very well, what's on your mind?"

Danny's heart was pounding, but he'd gone too far to turn back. "I think we should consider the possibility that someone in the department may be our killer."

It sounded unreal, even to Danny, and he held his breath as the lieutenant tilted back in his chair ever so slowly, his eyes fixed on Danny's. "That's a very disturbing charge, Detective. What led you to such a conclusion?"

"Well sir, there are several things that suggest a possible law enforcement connection."

The lieutenant's gaze flipped to the squad room, then back to Danny. "I'm listening."

Nervously, Danny started to lay out his theory, not stopping until it was all on the table. Kelly never interrupted him, keeping his stare locked on Danny. When he'd finished, the lieutenant tipped his head toward the ceiling and closed his eyes.

Finally, after several minutes, he rocked forward and fixed Danny with a stare that felt almost threatening. "I'm going to take what you've said under consideration. After I've had time to think it over, we'll meet again. Now, Sullivan..."

"Sir?"

"This conversation doesn't leave this room, understand?"

"Yes, sir."

"It never happened unless I say it happened, are we clear?"

"Perfectly."

"Okay. Thanks for coming to me. You're dismissed."

Danny quickly left the office, going straight to the bathroom. He splashed some water on his face, noticing his hands as he did. They were shaking too much to cover up.

He went into a stall and stayed there until he'd calmed down.

Well, the die has been cast. Let's hope it doesn't crush you.

Danny spent the afternoon reviewing all the details of the case. If the lieutenant agreed with his theory, and if he passed it on to Captain Walsh, Danny wanted to be prepared for the grilling sure to come.

Even more important, he wanted to defend himself against Murphy, who would probably feel blindsided again. Danny was counting on Murphy's understanding of the position he was in, not wanting to burn the wrong bridge, and unsure who to go to.

At least he hadn't called Michaels from IA.

Murphy was still working the gray sedan angle, hoping to find the needle in a haystack the size of Southie. He pulled the records of every gray four-door car licensed in South Boston and took them into the conference room.

Danny went in to check on his progress. "How's it going?"

Murph looked up at him with bleary eyes. "Well, I started whittling the pile down by taking out drivers by age—amazing how many gray sedans are owned by retirees—then I checked gender. I removed those registered to females, which got me to a small enough number that I could run background checks on the drivers whose ages fall into the FBI profile."

"Boy Murph, that sounds like fun!"

"You have no idea. How's it going with you?"

"I've reviewed every picture in both files, and I'm unable to find a single thing we've missed. I was getting ready to pull the prowler report from Saturday night and look it over."

Murphy looked up at the clock. It was already past four in the afternoon. "I guess I'll stay with this for another hour or so."

"Good luck."

Danny closed the conference door and returned to his desk. He pulled the report filed early Sunday morning by Kevin. It was short and to the point.

Sandra Cooper, age forty-six, had sensed she was followed home. When she got inside the house, she had gone to the bathroom, coming out a few minutes later.

Her front window was at the end of the hall, and she thought she saw a man standing off to the side, next to a fence that separates her yard from her neighbor's.

She dialed 9-1-1 while trying to get a better look. Less than five minutes after she hung up with the operator, the man disappeared around the edge of the fence. Miss Cooper had called her neighbor to find out if she'd also seen the man, but the neighbor was asleep.

The description was vague and no vehicle was seen.

To Danny, one detail stood out over everything else. The man disappeared soon after the call to 9-1-1.

Does that support the idea of a law enforcement connection? Or did the man just happen to see her on the phone?

It could be either, and a fifty-fifty possibility was not the kind of corroboration he was looking for. He needed more.

He stood and stretched, noticing Murphy had left the conference room. Assuming his partner was getting ready to call it a day, Danny headed for home.

****

The conference door opened, and when Murphy looked up, he was surprised to see the lieutenant waving at him. When he went to say something, Kelly held a finger to his lips, then spoke in a hushed tone. "My office before you go home."

Murphy nodded, uncomfortable with the secrecy. It was out of character for the lieutenant.

Did Sullivan say something? Maybe Marcus just wants to talk about his wife some more.

He'd had enough for one day anyway, and closed up the files before going to Kelly's office. Once inside, he shut the door and dropped into a chair. "What's up, Marcus?"

Marcus stood and closed the blinds on the office door, then returned to his desk. "We have a situation."

"Oh?"

"It's Sullivan."

"What about him?"

"He came to me this morning with a new theory on the case you two are working."

Murphy sensed his blood pressure rising. "Is that so? What exactly was this new theory?"

"He thinks..." Kelly hesitated. "His suggestion is the killer may be one of our own."

Murphy stared at the lieutenant, careful not to say the wrong thing, despite an urge to tell Kelly precisely what he was thinking. "I see... What does he base this theory on?"

Kelly slid a single sheet of paper across the desk, remaining silent while Murphy picked it up and read the information. When he was done, Murphy threw the paper back on the desk. His voice dripped disdain. "Fascinating."

"I know you weren't aware of this, so I wanted your opinion."

"No you don't."

"I'm sorry?"

"You *really* don't want to hear my opinion, and I *really* don't want to share it."

Kelly stared at his detective for nearly a minute. Finally, he scooped up the piece of paper and put in a folder. "Very well. I'm going to consider how to proceed tonight, then we'll meet tomorrow."

"Fine. Is that all?"

The lieutenant nodded and Murphy stood. Throwing the door open, Murphy went in search of Danny. Unfortunately, the kid was already gone.

WEDNESDAY, NOVEMBER 17

SULLIVAN RESIDENCE
WEST ROXBURY
6:45 A.M.

Danny was finishing his breakfast when the phone rang. "Sullivan."

"This is Lieutenant Kelly. Are you on your way in?"

"Actually, I was just finishing breakfast."

"I need you in my office at 7:30. Can you make it?"

Danny looked at the clock on the wall. "Yes, sir."

"Good. See you then."

The line went dead. There was no mistaking the tone in the lieutenant's voice, and Danny's heart pounded as he began to think the worst.

"What's wrong with you? You look like you've seen a ghost."

He put down his phone and forced a smile. Cass had brought him a travel mug of coffee. "Nothing. That was the lieutenant saying he wants me to get a move on."

He got up, put on his jacket, kissed a startled Cass, and headed for the car. The suggested Nor'easter had shown up, and snow was starting to fall.

Normally, Danny would enjoy the season's first serious snowfall, but today, he barely noticed. His mind was already going over the different scenarios of his meeting with the lieutenant.

None of them ended well.

LIEUTENANT KELLY'S OFFICE 7:25 A.M.

Danny had thrown his coat over his chair on the way to the lieutenant's office. The door to the office swung wide and Murphy came out, nearly running Danny over. The younger detective managed to avoid the collision, but when Murphy saw him, they locked eyes. Outside the snow was falling hard and the wind was howling, but it was the chill in Murphy's look that sent a shiver through Danny.

Murphy's voice was more of a hiss. "I told you never to do that again."

For a moment, Danny thought his partner was going to take a swing at him, but Murphy turned on his heels and left. Danny had been holding his breath, and forced himself to exhale.

Shaken, he turned into the open office door. A grave-looking Lieutenant Kelly waved him in. "Close the door."

Danny did and took the nearest seat. "I gather you told Murphy my theory."

Kelly nodded. "I needed his opinion. I think you got a pretty good idea of how he felt."

Danny didn't respond, instead waiting for Kelly to get to the point.

"Detective Sullivan, I'm not happy about this, but I going to have to remove you from the Brennan-Nolan case."

Danny's heart was in his throat. "Because of my theory, sir?"

"Yes and no. While I do not agree with your assertions, you were doing your job to the best of your ability. I can't fault you for that, but it gets to the crook of the problem. You're too inexperienced for a case this... how should I put it... intricate."

"But sir..."

The lieutenant held up a hand. "Let me finish. There's also the issue of Murphy. I believe your working relationship with him is damaged beyond repair, at least in the short term."

"Sir, I know the case well, anybody else will have to get up to speed before they can make an impact."

"Perhaps, but I've put Timmons with Murphy, and he's had plenty of experience. I'm thinking a fresh set of eyes could be good for the case anyway."

"Respectfully sir, I request to stay on the case. I'll get the job done."

"Your request will be noted but the decision is made."

Danny was suddenly more angry than nervous. "Permission to speak freely, sir."

The lieutenant stared at him with furrowed brow. "Granted..."

"I can't help thinking my pointing a finger at this department may have something to do with your decision."

When Kelly answered him, it was slow, deliberate, and barely audible. "Are...you...suggesting a cover-up, Detective Sullivan?"

Danny's first thought was one he kept to himself. *If the shoe fits...*

"No sir, not that, but did my take on things somehow seem unreasonable?"

"No, not unreasonable, but incorrect. That is my job sometimes, to make the tough call."

"Yes, sir."

Kelly stood and opened the door, forcing a smile. "Look, go ahead and take the day off. Tomorrow, we'll talk and re-evaluate things going forward."

Danny recognized a lost cause when he saw one. "Very well, sir."

Back at his desk, he called his father. "Hello?"

"Pop, it's Danny."

"Oh, hi son. How's that case going?"

"Unfortunately, there's been some changes made by the lieutenant."

"I see..."

"I was wondering if I could take you to lunch."

"I'd be glad to, as long as the snow doesn't get too bad."

Danny had forgotten about the growing storm. "Well, maybe we can walk down the road to the Lincoln."

"That sounds good, see you around eleven?"

"Yeah... and Pop, thanks."

"No, thank you... You're buying!"

LINCOLN TAVERN
11:20 A.M.

Several inches of snow were on the ground already, and they had to shake off their coats at the door to keep from snowing on everyone they walked past. The small pub was less than half full, and they were seated immediately at a table next to the large front window.

The gray sky matched Danny's mood, but his father was doing his best to keep things light. "How about a Guinness?"

"Sounds good, but are you allowed?"

Pat Sullivan made an exaggerated look over both shoulders and then out the window. "I don't see your mother, do you?"

Danny smiled in spite of his mood. They ordered food to go with their drinks and the tall glasses arrived a short time later. After clinking mugs and wiping the foam from their top lips, the elder Sullivan focused on his son. "So, let's hear it."

Danny took another swig. "The lieutenant removed me from the case this morning."

"I see... and what were his reasons?"

"Well, let's see. First, he said I was too inexperienced for a case so 'intricate.' Then, he said my working relationship with Murphy was damaged beyond repair."

"I gather you shared your theory of the case with Kelly."

"Yesterday. He said he didn't agree with it, then called it incorrect."

Pat sipped his beer. "I can't say I'm surprised."

"I guess if I'm honest, I'm not either."

"Did he say whether his decision had anything to do with your theory?"

Danny was slowly spinning his half-empty glass. "I asked him that. His response was to ask me if I was suggesting some sort of a cover-up. I hadn't anticipated that."

"No, I would guess not. Seems to be a bit of a leap."

"I thought so. Anyway, it's a done deal. He put Timmons on the case with Murphy."

Pat finished his drink just as their lunch arrived and ordered another round. "Do you still think your theory holds water?"

"I do. In fact, there was another prowler report that fit the pattern."

"Then, if any further discussion comes up, you stick to your guns. You can't be seen as caving to pressure. Follow your gut—it's the best investigative tool you have."

Danny now looked at his father in a different light since the conversation with his mother. Pat Sullivan would have been a great detective, if he'd wanted to.

Danny raised his glass. "Here's to following your gut!"

They clinked mugs, and Pat added his own toast. "And if you can't, here's to filling it with Guinness!"

They clinked again, laughing as they drank. Outside the big window, snow was beginning to really pile up, but it didn't seem to matter anymore.

THURSDAY, NOVEMBER 18

PRECINCT C-6
8:30 A.M.

Danny's mother had driven him home from the lunch with his father, and so Danny had to take a taxi to get his car the next morning. As a result, he arrived at the station later than he'd planned. The snow had stopped overnight, leaving nearly two feet on the ground, but the street crews had done their job. The roads were passable.

After hanging up his coat, he went to his desk, hoping Murphy would be there. He wanted a chance to explain why he hadn't filled Murphy in. It wasn't that he didn't want his partner to know what he was thinking, he just wasn't sure how to tell him.

Danny didn't want Murph to think he considered him a suspect, even though it was sure to come across that way.

Unfortunately, Murphy and his new partner were nowhere around. Neither was the lieutenant. Since he had no assigned task, he saw no reason he couldn't spend the morning trying to help Murphy with the case they had shared. Danny had gone over the files multiple times, but there was one thing he hadn't re-examined—the bus video.

He sat down at his desk and logged into his computer. Accessing the copies in the video databank, he brought up the on-board cameras from Cary Brennan's ride home on the night she disappeared. He started them moving forward, very slowly, something he hadn't been able to do the day he and Murphy had watched the videos at MBTA Central.

The video from the first leg of Miss Brennan's trip was uneventful and nothing new popped out. Danny called up the second one, this one running from Andrew Station to Brennan's stop near her home. Again, he moved the pictures forward slowly, and again he saw nothing new.

Frustrated, he started the process over, and then a third time. The pictures were in color but grainy. Nevertheless, he could make out the faces and clothing of each person. He was finished with the third time through the tapes, but before starting over, he let the last one run a little longer.

What was that?

He backed the tape up and let it run. A light-colored flash went past the bus. It was barely visible over the driver's shoulder, but it was there. Danny backed the tape up again, but this time, he watched it frame by frame.

His heart started to pound as the vehicle came into view, appeared for about six frames, then was gone. He backed it up, starting it forward frame by frame again, until it hit the fourth frame in the series. He froze the picture.

It was a four-door sedan, only feet from Cary Brennan on the night she disappeared, but it wasn't gray.

Silver! The car wasn't gray, it was silver!

Danny punched print on his keyboard, and retrieved the photo. The lieutenant was still not in, but Danny couldn't wait. He called Murphy.

"Lieutenant Murphy."

"Murph, it's Danny."

Chilly would be an understatement for his reaction. "What?"

"I was looking at the bus videos and I found something."

"I'm sure you did, but you'll have to take it to Lieutenant Kelly."

"But... don't you want to hear what it is?"

"I can't discuss the case with you any longer."

The phone went dead. Danny stared at the receiver, unable to make sense of what was happening.

He can't accept help? I have to take a lead through the lieutenant?

He set the phone down. If that was the way it was, then so be it. He'd wait for the lieutenant.

****

Danny waited nearly an hour and a half before Lieutenant Kelly finally showed up in the squad room. Once the lieutenant was in his office, Danny took the picture to him. "Sir?"

"Oh hey, Sullivan. I know we were supposed to talk this morning but I got caught up in something. Sorry about that."

"No problem. I spent the time going over some video and I found something."

Kelly dropped into his chair. "Found something?"

"On the bus video."

"What bus video?"

"From the Brennan case."

It was impossible to miss the tightening in the lieutenant's jaw. "Shut the door."

218

Danny reached over and swung the door closed. When he turned back, the lieutenant was seething. "Did I not make myself clear when I said you were off the case?"

"Yes sir, but..."

"What have you got?"

Danny slid the picture across the desk. "The gray vehicle referred to by one witness, and possibly confirmed by another...It wasn't gray. I believe the vehicle in this picture is the one we're looking for, and it's silver. Murphy needs to be doing a records search on silver, not gray, sedans."

Kelly picked up the photo, scanned it, then turned and laid it on a side table behind him. "I'll pass it on."

"They also need to watch for it on the surveillance detail."

"There is no detail. It's been cancelled."

Danny was stunned. "But I thought it was a proactive idea to safeguard Jennifer Morris."

Marcus Kelly stood, leaning toward Danny, both hands on his desk. His fixed his young detective with a penetrating glare. "I'm going to say this one last time. Leave the Brennan-Nolan case alone! I am giving you an order, and if it is disobeyed, your time in this unit will be over. Are we clear?"

"Yes, sir."

"Now get out of my office and out of the precinct for the rest of the day."

Danny left without uttering another word. The door slammed behind him, and several detectives looked up from their desks, a knowing smirk on their faces. Danny grabbed his coat and left the station without slowing down.

SULLIVAN RESIDENCE
WEST ROXBURY
12:15 P.M.

Danny's appearance at the front door was cause for celebration in Cassie's eyes. "You're home for lunch. That's awesome!" His muted reaction immediately tempered her enthusiasm. "What's wrong?"

He took off his coat and went to the couch, dropping down in a demonstration of the exhaustion he felt. "I had a run-in with Lieutenant Kelly."

She came over to him and sat down. "What happened?"

"Well, let's see. I told him I suspected somebody in law enforcement may be responsible for the deaths in the case I was working. He took it under consideration for less than twenty-four hours, then removed me from the case."

"What? You're kidding?"

He shook his head slowly, staring down at his hands. "I wish I was. It gets better."

"Better or worse?"

"Better in a sarcastic way."

"So worse. How?"

Danny looked up at her but had trouble meeting her gaze. "I had some time to kill this morning, so I did a little more investigating on the case. I found a lead for Murphy to follow up on, but when Kelly found out, he went ballistic."

"Oh Danny, I'm sorry... Did he fire you?"

"No, at least not yet. He made it pretty clear my days were numbered if I disobeyed his orders again."

"How convinced were you about it being a cop?"

"Plenty. I still am."

She leaned over and kissed him. "Then I don't care what happens. I'm glad you did what was right."

He looked up into her eyes. "Thanks. That means a lot."

She stood up. "So, since you're here now, can I assume you have the rest of the day off?"

He nodded and she turned toward the kitchen. A few moments later, she returned with two steaming bowls of something that smelled wonderful.

"Lunch is served, Detective. And my orders for you are to enjoy the afternoon with your very pregnant wife."

Danny smiled. "That's the kind of order I can follow!"

FRIDAY, NOVEMBER 19

SULLIVAN RESIDENCE
WEST ROXBURY
2:33 A.M.

Danny rolled over and looked at the clock. He couldn't sleep, not because he wasn't tired, but because his mind wouldn't shut off. Something was wrong, he could feel it. But it wouldn't come together for him.

It was as if the pieces of a jigsaw puzzle were whirling around him in the air. When he was able to get several pieces pinned down on the table, he had no picture to work from. The clues were all around him, but he couldn't make them fit together because he didn't know what the picture was supposed to look like.

He checked on Cassie, who appeared to have dozed off, and climbed out of bed. Throwing a robe on against the chill, he went into the kitchen and poured himself a glass of milk, then grabbed a pen and paper from the junk drawer.

Okay, now that you're up in the middle of the night, how do you make sense of all this? Starting with the idea that a cop is responsible, who fits the bill? Most have the knowledge to commit crimes with clean scenes, but what else?

He tore off three sheets of paper. At the top of the first, he wrote:

Murphy
1. No known motive or connection to victims
2. Responded to at least two prowler reports
3. Was out of town during Lisa Nolan murder
4. Not on surveillance detail when prowler report filed on S. Cooper
5. No silver car

On sheet two:

Kevin
1. Responded to multiple calls involving prowlers
2. Was first to the Lisa Nolan scene
3. Does not own silver car
4. No known motive or connection to victims

Finally, on sheet number three:

Duffy
1.   Found Cary Brennan body
2.   Responded to multiple prowler calls
3.   No known motive or connection to victims
4.   No...

He stopped.
Duffy showed up at Cary Brennan's funeral in a silver car!

He scratched out the "No" and put silver car for point number four.

Still, Duffy and how many other thousands of people have silver cars?

Danny lined the sheets up across the table in front of him. The longer he stared at them, the dumber he felt. He'd brought a ton of trouble down on himself, and when he looked at the sheets, he could see why he was alone in his conviction. It wasn't exactly overwhelming evidence.

He didn't make a separate list, but it occurred to him that six other officers showed up on the prowler reports. Perhaps he'd been too quick to rule them out. He would run their names the next day. Still, as he looked at his notes, he realized it was something other than these few facts that was bothering him.

225

What? Come on, Danny-boy! What is it?

He went back over the last couple weeks, beginning with the first day of the Brennan missing persons case. As he tracked through each day, he found his suspicion growing, but the unease he felt didn't come to a head until he spilled his theory to the lieutenant.

Everything changed. The entire feel of the case was different, but why? Was it just because Kelly was angry? Or was it because he was threatening?

Danny stood and started pacing around the living room.

Lieutenant Kelly was the one who had really changed the investigation. He pulled me off the case. He cancelled the surveillance. He ordered Murphy not to discuss the case further with me.

Danny rubbed his temples, trying to fight back a headache that was intent on torturing him.

Think! Think! What is your gut telling you?

Danny stopped dead.

He's protecting someone!

Walking back over to the papers on the dining table, he hunted for answers.

The first question is who. One of these three or someone else?

*The second question is why? Loyalty,
debt to someone, a friend?*

"What are you doing?"

Danny jumped, clutching his heart.
"Oh... Cass, you scared me."

"The feeling is mutual. I woke up and
someone was walking around my house."

He went to her, wrapping his arms
around her shoulders. "Sorry. I couldn't
sleep."

"The case?"

"Yeah."

"You're going to ruin your career if you
don't let it alone."

"That won't happen, I promise."

Cass shook her head and went back
down the hall to the bathroom. When she
came out, she stopped and called to him.
"Coming to bed?"

"Yes. Be there shortly."

He took a final look at the sheets before
putting them away.

*Find who Lieutenant Kelly is protecting
and I'll find the killer.*

PRECINCT C-6
7:02 A.M.

The next morning, Danny was at the station before anyone else on the day shift. The night officers were still filing their reports from the previous shift, but the Major Case squad room was empty. He quickly ditched his coat and sat down at his computer.

First, he pulled up the names of the other six officers from the prowler reports. One at a time, he ran a search of the Massachusetts Registry of Motor Vehicles. None of the them had a silver car registered to them.

Next, he ran Jack Duffy through the MRMV, which popped up a silver Toyota Camry.

Strike one against Jack. But why would Kelly protect him?

There was no connection between the two that he was aware of. He pulled up the bus photo he'd printed off for the lieutenant, and though it wasn't anywhere near a positive ID, there was nothing to suggest it couldn't be Duffy's car.

"Sullivan!"

Danny punched the escape button on his keyboard, startled he was no longer alone. "Sir?"

Lieutenant Kelly was staring at him from about ten feet away, the suspicion on his face obvious. "What are you doing?"

"Sir?"

"Do you have anything going right now?"

"No, sir."

"Good. I want you on the pistol range today. Brush up and re-qualify."

"Yes, sir."

The lieutenant went into his office, closing the door behind him. Danny fought the frustration building inside.

Couldn't be a better place to get someone out of your hair!

As Danny headed down to the basement, he ran through his options.

If I'm gonna prove he's protecting someone, I'm gonna have to have evidence of why. And if I'm going to save Jennifer Morris and Sandra Cooper, it better be soon.

Danny was aware both Kelly and Murphy liked to take their weekends off, and with the surveillance detail cancelled, they were even less likely to be at the precinct.

229

I need access to the lieutenant's office, so Saturday will have to be it. Sunday might be too late.

The rest of the day was spent at the range, not because it took that long, but because Danny didn't want to find out what the lieutenant had in mind for him to do next.

That evening at home, Danny purposely avoided any discussion about work. It seemed to suit Cassie just fine.

SATURDAY, NOVEMBER 20

PRECINCT C-6
_9:05 A.M._

Danny had purposely timed his arrival at the station to be after the night shift had gone home, and the day patrol was already on the streets. There was only one person in the Major Case squad room; Detective Timmons.

Danny threw his coat on the back of his chair, reached over and dialed his own cellphone. When it started to ring, he hung up the desk phone and "answered" his cell.

"Sullivan." He picked up a file folder and walked toward the conference room. "Hey, Dad. How's Mom?"

Inside the room, he spread the contents of the file folder out on the table, then returned to the door, continuing his ruse. "Are you going to watch the Bruins' game?"

Danny positioned himself outside the room, leaning against the wall so he could see into Kelly's office. "Sean gonna be able to make it?"

From his vantage point, he began to look over the lieutenant's office. Starting with the desk, he tried to see each exposed piece of paper, each file folder, and every report. Nothing stood out.

Timmons got up from his desk, put on his jacket, and headed for the elevator. Danny nodded to the detective, who returned the gesture.

The floor number above the elevator lit up, followed by a "ding" and the doors sliding open. Timmons climbed on and was gone.

Danny put his phone away and continued his scan of the office for something that wasn't right. A book or picture, anything that may have been removed or replaced. The office was a meticulous as ever and nothing stuck out.

Well Danny, that was the easy part. Now we find out if you've got the chutzpah to follow your gut.

He checked the elevator one more time, and went into the office. Starting with the desk drawers, he went through each one. Nothing caught his eye. Next, he went to the file cabinet and ran his fingers across the file tabs in each drawer. Again, nothing stood out.

There were two drawers in the side table behind the desk, and he crossed to it, taking a quick look at the elevator. No lights. He was just about to open the top drawer when his mind flashed back to the day he'd sitting there trying to figure out what was missing.

The picture of Kelly and his wife. It should be right here.

He quickly looked around the room to see if it had been moved, but didn't see it. Reaching down, he opened the top drawer, finding just a Boston phone book. However, when he opened the bottom drawer, he froze.

Staring up at him was the picture of Lieutenant Kelly and his wife. Danny slowly lifted it, not sure he believed his eyes. The Lieutenant's wife was nearly as tall as her husband, with large, dark eyes, a bright smile, and dirty-blonde hair.

Danny thought he might vomit.

It can't be.

"DING"

Danny's attention jumped to the elevator. The doors were just starting to open. Without time to think, he raced across the office and pulled the drawstring on the blinds. Pinned next to the wall, he looked toward the still open office door.

If it was Kelly who just got off the elevator, Danny was pretty sure he would have to fight his way out of that office, especially because of the picture still in his hand.

He started to feel faint and realized he was holding his breath. He forced himself to take in air as the sound of someone moving around the squad room grew louder. Finally, he pulled the edge of the blind back enough to see who it was.

Murphy!

Danny let go of the blind, and weighed his options if he was discovered.

Should he show him the picture or take it to the captain? Maybe Murphy is helping Kelly. Besides, what did the picture really prove? It might just be coincidence.

"DING"

Danny peaked out from behind the blind again, this time to see Murphy getting back on the elevator. When the doors closed, Danny sucked in a huge breath. Rushing to the side table, he put the picture back, and got out of the office.

Back in the conference room, he gathered up the folder and its contents before returning to his desk. He needed something more than just that picture to go on, and in an instant, he knew what it was. He grabbed his coat and headed down to the main entrance.

FRONT DESK
PRECINCT LOBBY
10:10 A.M.

There is only one way into the precinct for the public; through the front lobby. Officers and their prisoners were admitted through a side parking garage, but no one else.

The first thing someone encountered when they came in the precinct doors a was semi-circle desk manned by an officer. In front of him was an array of video screens, which gave the desk constant feedback on what was going on throughout the entire station.

Sergeant O'Leary, someone Danny had known since he was a boy because of his father, was on duty. Danny grinned at him and extended his hand. ""What are you doing here on a Saturday?"

O'Leary grabbed Danny's hand and pumped it vigorously. "It's my switch for getting Thanksgiving Day off."

"I see. Seniority has its perks, doesn't it?"

The officer grinned. "Sometimes, but it usually just means we need put out to pasture soon!"

Danny laughed. "Come on, now! You've got at least one good month left in you."

O'Leary shook his head. "Really? Kick a guy when he's down?"

"Learned it from my dad."

"Well, if you learned how to be a cop from him, you'll do fine."

Danny moved around behind the desk. "Can you do me a favor?"

"I'll try. What's up?"

"How far back does the video for these cameras go?"

"At least thirty days. Why?"

Danny gave the sergeant sheepish grin. "Well, it's not police business, exactly."

"What then?"

"I ordered a Christmas present for Cassie and had it sent here. UPS said it was delivered, but I never got it. I want to see if I can verify the delivery."

"Sure, no biggie. What day did they claim it was dropped off?"

"Well, they said the station is on the end of the route and it was late in the day, say around six. They say the problem is they can't read the signature. The date on the slip was October twenty-eighth."

"Okay, let's pull it up." The sergeant pushed several computer keys, spun a wheel, then hit play. "This is the front door camera from four that afternoon."

Danny watched the images move forward at a slightly enhanced speed, but he wasn't looking for a UPS driver. If the lieutenant had been telling him the truth, Lisa Nolan should be on this camera. They watched until almost six-thirty. No driver, no Lisa.

O'Leary stopped the playback. "Looks like they stiffed ya."

"Maybe they have the date wrong. Can you try the day before and after for me?"

"Sure thing."

He repeated the playback on both days, the Wednesday before and Friday after. The result was the same. Lisa Nolan had not come to the station when Kelly said she had.

Danny thanked his friend. "I guess they have some explaining to do. I'll call them when I get home."

"Good luck."

Danny headed back to the squad room, his mind spinning.

Is the person who Kelly has been protecting... himself?

Back at his desk, he ran a check on Marcus Kelly through the MRMV. Registered to the lieutenant was a four-door Ford Taurus. He ran his finger across the screen to the color.

237

Silver!

He shut down the computer.

Another coincidence or solid proof?
You're gonna have to decide, Danny-boy.

SULLIVAN RESIDENCE
WEST ROXBURY
1:00 P.M.

He got home just after Cassie finished eating lunch, but the soup was still warm on the stove. He filled a bowl and joined her on the couch. She looked very uncomfortable. "*Your* child is kicking the crap out of me today."

He reached across and laid his hand on her stomach. Three quick thumps followed. "Wow, he is active. Maybe he wants to come out."

"Well, I'm not the one stopping him. Or her."

Danny smiled. "I wish I could carry him, or her, for you. Just to give you a break."

"That's very sweet, but no you don't."

Danny laughed. "Okay, maybe not. Do I still get the brownie points?"

238

She lifted his hand from her stomach and kissed it. "Of course."

He finished his soup and set the bowl on the coffee table. Cassie lay down and put her bare feet on his lap. Danny turned the TV on and found the Boston College game. Rubbing her feet gently while he watched, her breathing soon became regular.

He continued to massage as she slept.

****

For dinner, Danny went out and got Chinese food. It wasn't something they ate regularly, but Cassie was in the mood. "Besides, I've tried every other food that's supposed to start labor!"

When they were done, he finally brought up the subject he'd avoided all day.

"I've got some surveillance to do tonight."

"What? Now you tell me?"

"Well... It's not department surveillance."

Her stare turned suspicious. "What do you mean by that?"

"I'm doing some surveillance on my own."

"Danny..."

"Now, before you get mad, Cass, I want you to know it's very important."

"You're following somebody, aren't you?"

Danny hadn't married her because she was stupid. "Yes, but..."

"Who?"

"Lieutenant Kelly."

She looked at him as if he'd lost his mind, which he may have. "Daniel Sullivan! Why would you do a dang-fool thing like that?"

"Cass, I think he killed those women."

"What women? The one's from the case you were told to leave alone?"

"Yes."

"Danny, do you realize what you're suggesting? If you get caught, you could lose not just your detective badge, but your career!"

"I won't get caught."

She stared at him in silence, anger mixed with shock. He reached for her hand but she pulled it away.

"Cass, I have to do this."

"Why? Why do you have to put your job and our livelihood on the line? Why do you have to risk our baby's future on this?"

"Because...if I don't...another woman will die. I'm sure of it."

He could see her weighing his words against her emotions. "Why are you so sure?"

Danny laid out the basics, just the major points that had convinced him. When he was done, he waited. Cass got up and went to the kitchen, returning with a glass of water.

She stood looking down at him. "If you're wrong, Danny, and you get caught, all the repercussions won't just be on you. They'll impact your father and grandfather, as well. Have you considered that?"

He hadn't, and it made the decision even tougher, but he wouldn't back down now. "I have to do what my gut tells me, Cass."

She shook her head. "It's on you. I'm not going to discuss it any further."

Heading toward the bedroom, she left Danny alone in silence.

CITY POINT NEIGHBORHOOD
11: 15 P.M.

The bedroom door was closed when Danny went to leave, and he decided not to force the issue. He didn't like the earlier confrontation with Cass, but it hadn't changed his mind. One thing kept running through his head: how would he live with himself if he was right, and he let a murder occur he could have prevented.

He also struggled with the thought of hurting those he loved with his choices.

It was not a happy place he found himself in.

You better hope you're right, Danny-boy!

Swallow Street was more of an alley than a street, a one-way road running just a single block between N and O Streets. He parked near the intersection of Swallow and O, where he could see all activity coming and going.

A check of his watch told him he was early. It was just 11:15, and with the temperature hovering around freezing, he had to leave the car running. Cutting all the lights, including turning his dash lights to their lowest setting, he opened his thermos, poured some coffee, and slumped down in his seat to wait.

Marcus Kelly sat in his car, parked across the street from his home, just like he had most nights since being separated from his wife. He didn't like where he was staying, especially because it reminded him of her.

Eventually, the lights would go out in the house, and he would start to get sleepy. Despite dreading it, he would leave his long-time home behind, and go to his new quarters. Tomorrow, the routine would start over.

He pulled out of his parking spot, waited until he was past the house, and turned on his headlights. At the end of Swallow, he turned right and headed toward the waterfront.

Danny was just about to open the thermos for his second cup of coffee when a set of headlights flashed on, coming down Swallow. He put the thermos down, waited for the car to go by him, then checked the model.

Silver Taurus. Here we go.

Waiting until the car made a right on O Street, he pulled out and followed. When Danny turned onto O, he picked up the lieutenant's car about a block away, headed toward the waterfront. At William Day

Boulevard, they headed south, parallel to the Old Harbor.

Several other cars made following at a safe distance easy, and for nearly two miles they drove with the water and Harborwalk on their left. Eventually, they moved away from the waterfront and around the perimeter of several complexes, including the JFK Library.

Traffic thinned as they headed back toward the water, then onto Grampian Way. Kelly turned the silver Taurus into a parking lot that was unlit, and Danny decided it was too risky to follow him in. Continuing past the lot, he came to a large sign.

The Dorchester Yacht Club.

Danny's blood ran cold as the picture of the lone shoe print flashed through his mind.

He parked and waited. The silver car never reappeared and Danny finally headed for home at 1:30 Sunday morning.

SUNDAY, NOVEMBER 21

SULLIVAN RESIDENCE
WEST ROXBURY
1:30 P.M.

Danny had slept in and missed mass with Cassie. She was quiet when she arrived home, but to his relief, not angry. She didn't hide in the bedroom but instead made some small talk. Eventually, she got around to asking. "How did it go last night?"

"I found him and followed him, but lost him down by the yacht club in Dorchester."

"Yacht club? What was he doing down there?"

"I don't know, but one of our few clues was a print from a boat shoe."

She seemed unmoved by the revelation. "Right off the top of my head, I can think of ten people who wear boat shoes."

He nodded. "Me, too. But it's another piece of the puzzle."

She changed the subject. "Your folks asked about you."

"Yeah? What did you say?"

"I told them you worked late. They wondered if we were going to come by for lunch, but I told them I didn't feel up to it."

"Me, neither."

They were quiet for a while, Danny watching TV while Cassie worked on the Sunday crossword. Eventually, she set it aside and forced herself off the couch. "I'm gonna lay down."

"Okay. You need anything?"

"No," she hesitated. "Are you going back out tonight?"

He nodded. "I have to."

"Be careful."

As she headed off toward the bedroom, Danny tried to decide if that was a warning or a threat. He opted to think she was worried about him.

CITY POINT NEIGHBORHOOD 11:00 P.M.

Danny had left early, after kissing Cass goodbye and promising again to be careful, so he could be in position by eleven. He took up the same spot as the night before, engine on, lights all down. It would turn out arriving early was a wise decision.

246

****

Marcus Kelly sat in his car, watching the familiar house again, this time with a stranger's vehicle in the driveway. It was the third time in four weeks he'd found the car at his house. The first time he'd seen it, he ran the plates. It belonged to a co-worker of his wife.

He'd always prided himself on being in control, but that was before.

Before he had suspected something was going on.

Before it had been confirmed.

Now, he found himself consumed with anger, frustrated at his inability to control her and at times, himself.

The lights went out on the second floor, and he considered breaking in and making a scene, maybe taking out his frustration on the man in *his* bed. He knew better; the protection order meant jail.

He started the car and pulled away from the curb.

The silver Taurus came down Swallow and turned right, just as it had the night before. Danny checked his watch before pulling out to follow. Eleven-ten.

They proceeded down O Street toward the harbor, and turned onto William Day Boulevard going south. There was more traffic than the previous night, and Danny fell behind. At K Street, he lost sight of the Taurus, not picking it up again until it was too late. Kelly had turned north.

Danny's pulse picked up as found the quickest place to turn around and follow. By the time he'd got back to K Street and headed in the same direction, there was no sight of the Taurus.

Think, Danny! Where's he going?

In his head, he followed K Street north until it struck him.

Telegraph Hill!

Danny floored it and headed for the home of Jennifer Morris.

He pulled the Taurus off the road and parked in the exact spot Sullivan and Murphy had used as their stakeout location. Turning off his lights, a light snow had

248

begun to fall, forcing him to turn the wipers on occasionally.

He glanced at his watch. Eleven-thirty.

She should be coming along any time, and the rage combined with excitement began to build inside. There was only one way he knew to release it. He felt his jacket pocket for his weapon, excited by its presence.

His watch read eleven-thirty-nine when he saw Jennifer Morris get off at her stop.

As she walked down toward him, she looked over her shoulder several times.

She's scared, like a deer being stalked by a wolf.

His pulse raced as he waited for the right moment.

Jennifer Morris kept her jacket pulled tight and her pace quick. Ever since the surveillance had been called off last week, she'd felt extremely vulnerable. The worse part of each day was the walk home from the bus stop.

In her hand, she kept a small container of pepper spray, but it gave her little comfort. She figured she was more likely to spray herself than an attacker. The light snow and deep cold meant she was alone. Nobody was out at this hour in these conditions.

She was halfway to her house when some headlights came on, followed by blue flashing emergency lights. Relief washed over her.

They must have re-started the surveillance without telling me.

A car stopped next to her and the window rolled down. "Jennifer Morris, right?"

She didn't recognize the officer, but smiled anyway. "Yes. Are you part of the team watching me?"

"I am," he got out of his car. "And I'm just checking to make sure you get home safe."

"Well, thank you... I'm sorry, I don't know your name."

He stepped toward her, something in his hand. "The name's..."

Suddenly, he lunged at her, wrapping his arm around her chest and turning her back toward him. He raised his hand to her throat as Jennifer cried out, but her scream was cut short by the blinding pain coursing through her.

As the pain subsided, she felt herself being dragged toward the open car door.

****

"Let her go, Lieutenant!"

Danny had his gun leveled at Kelly, his flashlight on the lieutenant's face. Kelly raised one hand, trying to shield his eyes. "Who's that?"

"Danny Sullivan."

"Sullivan! What are you doing?"

"I'm saving this woman's life. Release her and step away."

Jennifer wasn't moving and Danny worried he was too late. He put the flashlight down and grabbed the radio. "Dispatch!"

"Go ahead."

"Officer needs back-up at sixth and Webb Park!"

"Copy that!"

Marcus Kelly glared at the young detective. "Have you lost your mind?"

"Let her go, sir!"

Rage surged across the lieutenant's face and his voice dropped to a hiss. "I'll have your badge for this, Sullivan."

"Perhaps, sir. First, you'll have to explain why you attacked Miss Morris."

Jennifer started to come around and Danny took a step closer to the lieutenant. "Don't make this any harder than it has to be, Lieutenant! It's over."

Kelly laughed. "Over? What exactly do you think you've accomplished? Besides ending your career."

"You and I both know what just happened."

"Really? I was just checking on Miss Morris and found her collapsed on the sidewalk."

"That's not what I witnessed."

"It's your word against mine, Sullivan. Who do you think they're going to believe?"

"I guess we'll find out."

At that moment, a blue-and-white patrol car rounded the corner. Kelly looked at it, then at Danny. He dropped the girl and jumped into the open door.

Danny reacted instantly.

Throwing himself on the hood of the car, he aimed his gun through the windshield at the lieutenant's head. Kelly's hand was on the gearshift of the still running car as he glared at Danny, who returned it with one of equal intensity. "You twitch that hand and I'll pull the trigger!"

Kelly hesitated, not sure whether to test Danny's resolve.

Danny's glare didn't waver. "Turn the car off!"

Suddenly, Kelly's head swiveled to the side. Another person had joined the standoff.

"Do... as... the... man... said."

The gun of Sergeant Buckley was inches from Kelly's forehead. Marcus removed his hand from the gearshift and shut off the car. Buckley reached in and took keys. "Does someone want to tell me what is going on?"

Jennifer moaned and Danny went to her. "Are you okay?"

She was shaken and crying. "I think so."

Next to her on the ground was a Taser. Danny pointed at it. "There's your answer, Sergeant. Kelly used that on Miss Morris."

Buckley looked down at the weapon, then at Jennifer. "Is that right, ma'am?"

She was starting to become more clear-headed, and thrust her arm in the direction of the lieutenant. "That S.O.B. attacked me!"

The big sergeant reached into the car and jerked Marcus Kelly to his feet, slamming him onto the hood of the car. Once he was cuffed, Kelly was dragged in the direction of Buckley's patrol unit.

Danny got Jennifer up and took her to his car, putting her in the back seat. "You okay for a few minutes?"

She nodded, so he returned to the Taurus and popped the trunk. Buckley finished putting Kelly in the back his squad car, then joined Danny, shining his flashlight inside the compartment. "Oh, man. Think it's blood?"

Danny nodded. "Yes."

Leaving the trunk lid up, Danny went around to the passenger door. Inside, he pulled open the glove compartment. "Sergeant?"

Buckley came over. "Yeah?"

"You ever see anything like that?"

Buckley leaned over and peered into the box, shining his flashlight on a smooth leather object. "Not in a long time."

Danny looked up at him. "What is it?"

"A beavertail."

"A what?"

"It's actually called a Sap. It's a lead-filled piece of leather with a spring-loaded handle. The department outlawed them years ago."

Danny climbed back out of the car and retrieved his phone. Finding the business card in his pocket, he dialed the number and waited. "Hello?"

"Lieutenant Michaels?"

"Yes, this is Michaels."

"This is Detective Danny Sullivan. I think you should come down to my location."

"Why is that, Detective?"

"I just arrested Lieutenant Marcus Kelly for murder."

BOSTON HOMICIDE

MONDAY, NOVEMBER 22

PRECINCT C-6
4:30 A.M.

Danny had spent four hours being interviewed, filling out reports, and bagging evidence. When he'd arrived at the station, just after one in the morning, Captain Walsh, Murphy, Timmons, and a half-dozen other people he'd never seen before, were already in the Major Case squad room.

He wasn't sure what to expect, but so far, he hadn't received much in the way of acknowledgement for the arrest. Murphy was talking to him again, and Michaels was obviously impressed when she interviewed him, but Danny couldn't tell from the captain if he done something that in his eyes was good or bad.

To him, there was no question. Jennifer Morris would be dead right now if he hadn't followed his gut. He would thank his father for the advice.

Danny's phone rang. "This is Sullivan.!"

"Danny, it's me!"

"Cass... what is it?"

257

"My water broke!"

"What... When?"

"A few minutes ago. Your mom and dad are on their way. You need to meet me at the hospital."

"Okay, yeah. I'm leaving now. I love you."

"I love you, too. Hurry, okay?"

"I will."

Danny hung up and grabbed his coat. As he headed for the elevator, Murphy came out of the conference room. "Where are you going?"

Danny hit the elevator button, then opted for the stairs. "I have something to do."

"What?"

"Become a father!"

BOSTON MEDICAL CENTER SOUTH BOSTON 5:10 A.M.

A nurse held her hands up as Danny came barging onto the labor and delivery floor. "Whoa, whoa. Slow down there, fella."

"I'm sorry. My name is Danny Sullivan. My wife, Cassie, is here."

"Okay. Well, you're in plenty of time. She's in room 315 at the end of the hall."

"Thanks."

Danny walked down to the room and knocked lightly on the partially closed door. "Come in."

He found Cassie sitting up in bed and his mother sitting in a chair by the wall. Several monitors beeped while lines and numbers scrolled across multiple screens. He rushed to Cass and wrapped her in a hug. "I was so worried I wouldn't make it in time."

She smiled up at him. "Me too, but my labor is progressing slowly."

"Are you and the baby okay?"

"Fine..." Cass grimaced and grabbed the bedrail.

Danny looked to his mother. "Is she okay?"

"It's just a contraction. She's fine."

Danny stood by until Cass breathed with relief, then went around and hugged his mom. "Thanks for getting her here."

"Of course, dear. Your father went to get your grandfather."

"Has anyone called Sean or Bree?"

"Not yet. It could be hours still, and they can't get here anyway, so why get them up so early."

"Makes sense."

Danny dropped into a chair by the bed. Cass reached out and took his hand. "You were out all night."

He'd completely forgotten about the events at the station. "Cass... I was right."

Tears welled up and she squeezed his hand. "Are the women safe?"

Part exhaustion, part relief overwhelmed him and tears flowed down his face. "Yes."

****

At 12:34 p.m., Danny and Cassie were crying again, but this time for a different reason. The doctor had just held up their baby. "Congratulations, it's a boy!"

The nurses wrapped up their son and put him on Cassie's chest, where Danny could lean over and kiss his cheek. They laughed, then cried, then laughed again.

When Cassie was cleaned up, grandmother, grandfather, and great-grandfather were allowed in. The tears and laughter started all over again, this time with pictures.

His mother looked at Danny, joy beaming from her. "Did you have a name picked out?"

He looked at Cassie, who nodded her agreement. "Daniel Patrick Francis Sullivan."

His mother's eyes brimmed. "It's wonderful."

Danny couldn't remember ever being happier than he was at that moment.

BOSTON HOMICIDE

TUESDAY, NOVEMBER 23

SULLIVAN RESIDENCE
WEST ROXBURY
11:30 A.M.

Danny Jr. had arrived home an hour earlier. Both mother and baby were sleeping, which Danny had already begun to realize was not going to happen very often for the next while. He was on the couch with his grandfather, each with a cold Guinness in their hand, despite the early hour. Mom and Dad were due later.

Danny studied his grandfather.

Frank noticed and gave him a sideways glance. "Something on your mind?"

"Can I ask a personal question?"

"Fire away."

"Did you ever apply to be a detective?"

His grandfather's brow furrowed as he considered his answer. "That's kinda out of the blue, isn't it?"

"Maybe. I don't mean to pry..."

"No."

"No what?"

"No, I never applied."

This time, Danny *wasn't* surprised. He'd begun to suspect as much. "Can I ask why?"

His grandfather smiled at him. "Dinner."

"I'm sorry?"

"Dinner was the reason I never applied."

The confusion was evident on Danny's face. "I guess I don't understand."

"I wanted to be home with your grandmother every night for dinner."

Danny laughed. "Oh, now I get it."

Frank took a sip of his beer. "It wasn't that I didn't think I would enjoy the job, nor was it because I thought it was too difficult. It was because I didn't want police work to be my life." He took another sip. "I wanted my family to be my life."

Danny sipped his own beer. "Do you have any regrets?"

His grandfather smiled. "What do you think?"

"Well, I know if I was you, I wouldn't."

Frank nodded and grinned. "You're nearly as smart as your grandfather!"

****

Later that afternoon, his father and mother made it to the house. Pat Sullivan came through the door and pointed at his son. "You're a great one for news!"

Danny got up to get his dad a beer. "What are you talking about?"

"Captain Walsh called to congratulate me on raising such a fine son and officer. Needless to say, I appreciated the call, but then I asked him what prompted it."

Danny wasn't sure if his father was angry or just excited. "I guess he told you."

His father came over and hugged him. "I'm dang proud of you, Son."

Danny was moved by his father's reaction. "Thanks Pop. Your advice was what kept me going."

"Well, naturally, I assumed some of the credit was mine!"

Aileen punched her husband's shoulder. "Get out of the way, you old blowhard. Let me hug my hero son."

"Hero is overdoing it, I think."

"Not in a mother's book, it's not."

Cassie and Danny Jr. came out from the bedroom, immediately shifting all attention to the new baby. That suited Danny just fine.

The phone rang and Danny answered it. "Hello?"

"Congratulations, brother!"

"Thanks, Sean."

"I want a cigar when I get up there."

"You got it. When will you be here?"

"Tomorrow night. I'm picking up Bree, and we'll be in for Thanksgiving."

"Great. I can't wait to see you."

"Same here, but of course, I'm really coming to see my nephew."

Danny laughed. "Well, of course..." The phone beeped in his ear and he looked at the screen. "Bree is calling, I'll talk to you later."

"Good enough."

Danny hit the button to change calls. "Hi, sis."

"Hi, Danny Senior!"

"That sure sounds funny. I don't feel like a senior."

"Well, you are from now on. I only have a moment but I'll see you, Cass, and the baby tomorrow night."

"Can't wait. Bye, sis."

"Love to Cass. Bye."

Danny hung up, smiling to himself. *Family really is all that matters.*

WEDNESDAY, NOVEMBER 23
THANKSGIVING EVE

PRECINCT C-6
_8:45 A.M._

Even though he didn't have to be at the station on this day, Danny had a mission. When he got to his desk, a quick glance at Murphy's work area raised an alarm. It was empty, and all personal effects were gone.

Had Murphy been implicated? Was he part of it after all?

"Sullivan!"

Danny turned to see his old partner standing in the doorway to Kelly's former office. Murphy was waving at him. "Come on, I'll buy you a cup of coffee."

Danny went over to where Murphy stood, and followed him into the office. "Is there something I should know, Murph?"

"Oh, you mean about the office?"

"Yeah..."

"Well, it's just temporary, but it may become permanent."

"Have you been promoted?"

"No, but I have been instated as the temporary head of the Major Case Division."

"That's great, Murph. You deserve it."

Murphy looked genuinely touched. "What are you doing here, anyway?"

"I needed to talk to my superior, which is apparently, you."

Murphy laughed. "Just temporary for now. What's on your mind?"

"I want to be taken off the Major Case squad."

Murphy's surprise was evident on his face. He went and sat down in his desk chair. "Kinda sudden, isn't it? Can I ask why?"

"It's a personal thing. I don't think I want the hours. I'd prefer something a little more regular, with the baby and all."

Murphy studied his former partner, slowly rubbing his chin. "I've got an idea. Trust me?"

Danny laughed. "I guess."

"Shut the door."

Danny did while Murphy punched some numbers into his phone. It rang twice before the voice of Captain Walsh came on the line. "This is Walsh."

"Captain, this is Murphy. You're on speaker and I'm here with Danny Sullivan."

"Sullivan! How you doing, Danny? How's the baby?"

"Good, sir, thanks."

"The chief is gonna give you an award, did you hear that?"

"No sir, I hadn't. That's very kind of him."

"You deserve it. You took a nightmare situation for the department and turned it into a positive, at least as much as anyone could."

"Thank you, sir."

Murphy cleared his throat. "Captain, since I will be filling in here, I won't be able to accept your offer to join the Cold Case Unit."

"That's right. I'd forgotten about that."

"I'd like to put Sullivan forward for that opening."

"Sullivan! Murphy, that's a heck of an idea! Consider it done."

"Thank you, Cap." Murphy disconnected the call. "It's yours if you want it. Regular hours, very little if any night work, and you keep your rank."

Danny stood and shook Murphy's hand. "I owe you one, Murph. Thanks."

"You earned, Danny. Now go home to your wife and new baby."

"Yes, sir!"

SULLIVAN RESIDENCE
WEST ROXBURY
12:00 NOON.

Danny sat on the couch holding his son. He and Cass were alone with the baby for the first time since the day he arrived. Cass sat next to him, her gaze moving from her husband to her son, and back again. "He loves his daddy."

"His daddy loves him." Danny looked down at his wife. "I have something to tell you."

What he saw in her eyes was all the confirmation he needed for his decision. "Oh?"

"I stepped down from the Major Case Squad this morning."

She sat up, alarm on her face. "You aren't a detective anymore?"

"Well, I'm still a detective, but not in the same capacity. I accepted a position on the Cold Case Unit."

"What's that?"

"We look into unsolved cases and see if we can bring them back to life."

"Why did you do that?"

"You, this little guy, and dinner."

A quizzical smile crossed her face. "What are you talking about?"

He kissed his son's forehead. "I'll explain someday, but for now, just know this: I'll be home every night from now on."

"Seriously, Danny?"

He nodded and tears began a steady stream down her cheeks. She hugged his neck. "I love you."

"I love you, too." He smiled down at his son.

This is going to be a very good Thanksgiving!

****

A NOTE FROM THE AUTHOR:

I want to thank you for taking time to read *BOSTON HOMICIDE* and I hope you found it entertaining. It is my goal in each book to provide an enjoyable reading experience along with a little excitement.

This book is to be followed up by a series of similar works that stand alone in the city where they are placed. The next one

BOSTON HOMICIDE

on the planning board is *MIAMI HOMICIDE.*

Please don't hesitate to let me know how you felt about the book. I can be contacted at the links below.

God Bless, and thanks again for reading.

JOHN
I John 1:9

Cover by Beverly Dalglish
Edited by Samantha Gordon,
Invisible Ink Editing

MORE FROM JOHN C. DALGLISH

THE CITY MURDERS SERIES

BOSTON HOMICIDE - #1

MIAMI HOMICIDE - #2

CHICAGO HOMICIDE - #3

John C. Dalglish

THE DETECTIVE JASON STRONG
SERIES

"WHERE'S MY SON?" - #1

BLOODSTAIN - #2

FOR MY BROTHER - #3

TIED TO MURDER - #5

ONE OF THEIR OWN - #6

DEATH STILL - #7

LETHAL INJECTION - #8

CRUEL DECEPTION - #9

LET'S PLAY - #10

HOSTAGE - #11

CIRCLE OF FEAR - #12

DEADLY OBSESSION - #13

THE CHASER CHRONICLES

BOSTON HOMICIDE

Made in the USA
Middletown, DE
31 January 2019